KELLEEN GOERLITZ

Consumed by a Season

KelleenGoerlitz
Milwaukee, Wisconsin

First published by KelleenGoerlitz 2022
Milwaukee, Wisconsin

First edition

ISBN: 978-0-578-37994-4

Cover art by Hannah Goerlitz

This book was professionally typeset on Reedsy. Find out more at reedsy.com

The storyline for this book was inspired by a woman I'll never know. The glimpse I was given into her life resulted in a story bursting forth from my mind. It was a story of people who walk through postpartum with thoughts and feelings they never imagined having. It was her story, my story, a family member's story, a friend's story - maybe, your story. This book is for all of us.

Thank you Isidro, Hannah, Carlee & my mom for help completing this project and for always being there in my journey

Contents

III   Fall

IV   Winter

I

Spring

05/21/2012

"Is it important why?"

The question jolted him, bringing him back—from where, he didn't know. He rubbed his hand over his face, every part of his body feeling the emotional strain this conversation was having on him. He sat back on the couch, his vision slowly adjusting back to normal as the white spots from rubbing his eyes began disappearing. He looked at the calm brown eyes of the man across from him. The man's face was kind. That was one of the first things he had noticed about the man when he met him. He aspired to have a kind face too someday, even though the face he saw in the mirror was often worn and broken.

The man waited patiently for him to answer, his body comfortably still. He had on nice navy-blue dress pants and light brown loafers. The man's legs were crossed, his right foot hung comfortably and calmly.

His own foot automatically bounced.

"What was the question?"

"I asked if it was important why? Is it important why she left?"

Everything felt tedious—this question especially.

"I would think it should be." He regretted how gruff his response sounded in his ears. The kind face didn't deserve gruffness.

"Would it change your actions moving forward?" The man remained still. The room remained quiet. It could be peaceful.

"If it was because of me—then yes. If she left because of me, then I could do something different." His hand was back on his face as he leaned back into the couch, eyes toward the ceiling. He was tired of the conversation. He had been tired of the conversation for years. He was tired of thinking about her—of hating her—of loving her. He was even more tired of not knowing how to feel about himself.

The ceiling was a subtle gray while the rest of the room was painted white. He found that interesting.

"From our conversations over these past months, it seems like you are not currently causing any problems in your life. Do you feel like that's true or are you feeling differently? Is there something about you that needs to be different?" The man had uncrossed his legs and sat forward a little more, seeming drawn in by his own question—face still

4

calm, though with a hint of questioning.

Am I causing problems in my life? The question bounced around his head like an echo with nowhere to go. *Am I causing problems in my life?*

He thought about his daughter's face this morning as she sat at the kitchen table. The table was like a piece of art with all of its random divots, stains, and stray crayon marks he never bothered to wipe off. He didn't know if he just never took the time to really scrub it down, or if he purposely left it the way to encapsulate the life that had been lived at that table.

His daughter had been sitting at the table that morning as she usually did, with her tongue sticking out one side of her mouth in concentration, as the blue crayon in her hand swiftly moved across Arthur's face. The bowl of cereal next to her was apparently forgotten, until he asked her if she were boycotting cheerios. The green eyes slowly pulled themselves away from her masterpiece and her tongue slipped back into her mouth as she scrunched up her nose at him.

"What did a boy do to my cheerios?" she questioned with a mix of shock and confusion. A smile broke across his face which she instinctually mimicked.

"I asked if you were boycotting your cheerios. It means not doing something in the form of protest.

5

Like not eating cheerios to make a point." Her facial expression didn't change for a moment as her eyes stayed on him pensively. Then without moving her head, her eyes slid over to the bowl. With a quick movement, her blue crayon was abandoned, and her small hand wrapped around her spoon shoveling a heap of cheerios into her mouth with vigor. She then gave him the kind of smile only a five-year-old could, with her chin slightly lifted and her eyes mere slits—her cheeks filled with cheerios and milk. A suppressed laugh had escaped him as he sputtered into his coffee.

Am I causing problems in my life? He would often hear himself saying the words, "I just want her to be happy". They were said as a reflexive response to others and to himself at times. They were true—he wanted her to be happy. But he desperately wanted to be happy too.

"I think I've forgotten what makes me happy." The words seemed to just slip out. Startled, he found himself sitting up a little more, talking a little quicker as if his words would catch up to those already uttered and cover them up with alternative sound. "My daughter makes me happy. I am happy. I'm happy with her. I'm not saying I'm not." He saw that his slip had very subtly excited the man, who sat forward even more now as if getting closer to something.

"I know you love your daughter. You don't have to tell me that. Feelings of unhappiness and loving your daughter can coexist. They can live together in the same moment—in the same sentence. They don't negate each other." The man let his words rest in the air, hanging like a truth that would be breathed in. "Do you believe that can be true for you?"

He figured the man's words had the effect they were intended to. He felt his shoulders slightly drop as tension eased from his body—a tension born of guilt that had been gripping his insides for the past four years. "Yes"

"Do you believe that that could have been true for your wife?"

And there it was—the slap interrupting the calm. His body went into an instant boil, resulting in the physiological reactions he had become so accustomed to: hands and jaw clenched, the hum of his own blood in his ears, heart racing.

"It's completely different," he muttered, feeling his body close in on itself.

The man tilted his head in questioning.

"How so?" The man's face was innocently blank. It annoyed him. How could he not know the difference? He wasn't in the mood for the game—whatever therapeutic game it was.

"She left. She abandoned us. She could have let

me help her." His voice was loud and angry and he felt a twinge of embarrassment at the realization that he was essentially yelling at the man—the man with the kind eyes. Embarrassment wasn't enough to quell his outburst. He didn't care anymore—the anger fed him. Fuck it.

"Where do you get off saying that what I'm going through is the same as what she did?" Spit flew from his mouth, making the anger in his words even more tangible. The calm face didn't seem to notice. "She did this to us. She did it to herself. The only thing I did was try to help, try to understand, to support her. Love her." His voice cracked as he felt the intense energy begin to ebb away. The heaviness of grief pulled him back down. "She could have done something different." The tension in his body gave away out of exhaustion. "She didn't have to leave."

His gaze stayed resting on the floor slightly in front of his feet. Embarrassment became prominent in the de-escalation of his anger. He wanted to apologize, but something caught in his throat kept him from doing so. Maybe if he didn't apologize or acknowledge it, they could just move on—pretend the outburst didn't happen. He flinched as if flicked in the ear at the irony. It was just that kind of thought which landed him in therapy to begin with.

"Just so you know," the man replied lightly and

softly to his sudden silence, "I don't expect you to react as if we're having a casual conversation or as if the questions I'm asking are easy. I get to ask the questions and you get to respond. That's the deal. I get to choose the questions and you get to choose your response. And every response is justified if truthful."

Looking up at the man, he felt timid, as if he were a boy again looking up to see his father's face before being able to determine if everything truly was okay. The man's face was reminiscent of how someone looked coaxing a scared animal out of hiding. A few moments of shared eye contact seemed to reassure the man as he slightly readjusted his body, and the blank calm face was put back into place.

"Why do you think she didn't have to leave?" The question made his mind tense up in confusion, but the rest of his body was still tired and remained subdued.

"I—I'm not sure what you mean."

"From what we've discussed, she was generally a level-headed person, smart, caring, not prone to being overly selfish. So why do you think she didn't have to leave? You are assuming there was something else she could have done. Why not assume that in her mind, at that time, she truly believed that all she could possibly do was leave?

Why not assume that she did have to leave?"

He felt dumbfounded as the man's words hit him. He could feel his body tense and fall all at the same time, as if the systems within him heard two different things and fired appropriate reactions in unison. In his head, a steady stream of thoughts began to roar through: arguments, defenses, frustrations of all kinds. But he felt his heart soften as if suddenly allowed to rest from the anger and pain in the comforting hands of truth.

Feelings of unhappiness and love can live in the same moment.

She had loved them. Even though she had left them, she had loved them.

04/22/2002

The scent of closing time filled the air. The warm golden light bouncing off of the shining lacquered wood tables—gold accents all around the shop glimmered. She breathed in deeply, taking in the scent of coffee, faint smells of musk and cashmere coming from the few candles that were burning—all mixed along with the disinfectant she had in her hand as she wiped down the tables.

After a long day of the shop full of bustling customers, conversation and, every now and then, a moment of silence where everyone seemed to take a deep breath all at once—the sound at the end of the day was her favorite. It was the only time of day when all the notes of the music that played in the background could truly be heard, along with the echoes of all the words that had been carried upon other peoples' breath. During the day, the gentle thuds and clinks of cups on the wooden surfaces could be heard, but now there were only a few sporadic thuds as the last of the cups were dried and washed over at the bar.

Even though the shop contained only her and Jo, it was still so full. So full of all the echoes. So full of all the remnants others left. She breathed it all in—the dark charcoal walls; the wood tables carefully placed around the room, surrounded by chairs of black metal and leather cushions; the beautiful live-edge bar she was so excited for the day it was installed. Turning her head, she took in the rest of the magnificence. Cozy chairs sat together but in such a way that their occupants could feel totally separate or a part of those sitting along with them. Books that covered the walls were popular favorites and classics, but mostly works written by local authors. They sat up on the dark wood shelves waiting to be picked up by a patron. Everything was placed carefully along the walls, enough so that the eye was interested but also with enough space so the same eye wasn't overwhelmed. She remembered how much time they took picking out the right artwork, the right framed mirrors—feeling that each one had a special place along the walls.

A stronger *clang!* of a dish against the bottom of a sink brought her gaze over to the bar, which took up half of the room in its L-shaped formation. Behind it gleamed the silver of different coffee machines and a small oven. Shelves of shining glass coffee cups along with black matte clay mugs lined the wall, showing off in the recessed light glowing warmly upon them. Hanging lights over the bar area and throughout the shop gave off the same warm glow, making everything appear to be tinted with gold. Her hand grasped the cool metal of a chair which provided a subtle contrast to the warmth of her hand and the rest of the air.

She flipped the chair up onto the table taking enjoyment out of the smooth motion—a motion she had done every night for years. It had become a form of meditation to her—breathing in the echoes, feeling the warmth of the air fill her heart, and having her body flow in motion as one chair after another flipped from the floor to the tabletops. If there was anything in this world that she felt belonged to her, it was this place. Yet the best part about it was that it didn't belong to her at all, but rather to everyone who entered, grabbed a cup of coffee, and sat down to have their own moments known to her or not.

She remembered Jo's eyes when Jo had asked her to be a co-owner. Through many protests, she'd always decline the offer but told Jo that she would take on the dream with her—and she had. She had taken it on and it had become her own, making the coffee shop what it was today. She remembered all the different ideas that they had and the questions about what mood was to be set, what purpose was the coffee shop to have other than just filling people with caffeine. They had wanted a bar feel but then also acknowledged that some of the best moments were found in the silence of a comfortable bookstore or library chair—hearing the murmurs of people but being allowed to be in their own worlds as well.

"Should we do a bar atmosphere, or should we make it a place where people feel like they are at home or a home they wish they had?"

She remembered sitting on Jo's old couch—tapping her fingers on the plastic cup and Jo bouncing one of her legs—both of them taking sips of wine in silence waiting for the answer to find them. It had struck her, and she turned to Jo with the wonderment of simplicity.

"What if we do both?" she asked Jo with dumbfounded excitement.

The rest had just flowed. Within two years they had stood in their shop looking at the dream right there in front of them. It would have been inaccurate to say it materialized like magic as both of them had put as much of their time and effort into it as they possibly could—asking contractors to show them what easy, yet tedious, labor they could do themselves to cut down on costs. The day the different inspectors came out were days she didn't eat, and knew if she had, would have ended up vomiting on their shoes.

As she put up the last chair, she undid her hair and ran her fingers through it, enjoying nails on her scalp before tying it back up.

It started with just the two of them and a part-time employee who would fill in between college classes. Now they had a total of ten employ-ees—people who had been chosen not solely for their ability to do the job but who fit in with the family they had organically created for themselves. They were people who were skilled at reading others—recognizing patrons who enjoyed conver-sation with their coffee and those who appreciated familiarity and kindness but were looking for soli-tude among people. They were people who helped bring humanity to a building made of concrete, drywall and brick. It was as if over the years the walls had absorbed this, becoming less inanimate.

In the past year, they had prided themselves on sharing their successes and providing a place where independent bakers could sell their products, local authors' books were highlighted on the shelves, and the music of local musicians floated through the air from their speakers. Recently, they had even started getting their dairy products from farms in the nearby area, and a small rack of locally made honey sat on the counter by the checkout.

Jo had been so excited to give opportunity to other small businesses, rather than making any kind of expansion, when they realized they were actually making enough money to buy products for the shop, pay their employees well, provide benefits, and also give themselves a paycheck. The idea that they could do that and have extra money still shocked them.

As she sat down on a barstool, Jo instantaneously set a cup of coffee with a splash of sweet cream in front of her and pulled a bottle of Malibu out from the other side of the bar, adding a generous pour to her cup. Jo smirked as she poured her own and stashed the bottle back under the counter. They lifted their glasses in unison. It had been a tradition on nights they closed together, which was most nights in the beginning but had become more of a rarity in the last year.

Jo made her way around the bar, and they sat in silence for a moment, listening to the empty shop breathe, letting the warmth of the drinks settle in their chests.

"Did Devon tell you about his customer complaint today?" she asked Jo, smiling into her cup. Jo raised an eyebrow in surprise and slight confusion. Devon was one of their most thoughtful employees—taking customer service to a new level. People were pleasantly surprised by the twenty-three-year-old young man with designs shaved into the sides of his head and a tattoo on his neck. "Ms. Molly complained he was too ethical to flirt back with her, not giving into the deep connection she knows they're both aware of."

Jo gave her a classic snort of amusement and shook her head, laughing. They felt honored to have many regulars come into the shop almost daily—having found a home away from home. If anyone was the definition of a regular, it was Ms. Molly—a seventy-six-year-old witty woman with her own set of charming quirks, who seemed to have adopted the shop when they were open for about four months. She still remembered when Ms. Molly first entered the shop, her silk kimono filling the room with colors it was lacking—a dramatized gasp had been audible from the counter as Ms. Molly had surveyed her surroundings.

"Oh, this is just marvelous," Ms. Molly purred as she sat herself down at a barstool with a swoop of fabric and a glint in her eye. "Yes, it will do nicely!" She had been back every day since unless she was out of town on an adventure.

"Poor guy. When Ms. Molly picks a favorite, she picks a favorite," Jo said between chuckles. "Speaking of infatuation, how's that guy you've been seeing?"

Whenever anyone brought up her dating life

or relationship, she felt an automatic sense of annoyance. She didn't like processing such things out loud to people, uncertain of even how to, and she knew her uncertainty could leave the impression of a lack of investment or allow people to conclude for themselves the status of her current relationship. Sometimes processing her dating life made it apparent that something still existed that should have ended a long time ago.

She could hear her mother's voice telling her to stop wasting time on *so-and-so* kind of men, or *boys*, as her mother would put it with an air of insurmountable maturity. Even though she tried hard not to fall into the trap of feeling there was a ticking clock on finding a partner, becoming a family, having children, then winning the participation ribbon for ending up where the majority of other adults did—she could feel the presence of a small ball of anxiety in the pit of her stomach when it was brought up by others. In her gut, she knew that every moment of connecting with another—whether it was just a single date, some casual hookups, a short-term commitment—wasn't a waste of time. She would repeat that firmly to herself when the doubt crept in—the ticking cuckoo clock of anxiety projecting through her body

Despite all of this, Jo's question didn't send her

into a spiral of dread. If there was one person who she didn't feel confronted by—it was Jo. Jo was the kind of person who listened without judgment and didn't stop listening the moment she thought of something to say in response to something she heard. Jo didn't enter a conversation prepared to judge its contents—she was just in it for the sake of connecting.

"I think the guy I'm seeing isn't really who I want to be looking at anymore," she admitted staring down into her cup. A quick glance at Jo to see her reaction boosted her confidence in the thought she had voiced for the first time. Jo had given her a couple soft nods while taking another sip, knowing that additional questions were not necessary to get a further explanation. She took a short breath and continued.

"I'm finding myself wanting to just spend more time doing things by myself instead of with him. And I really don't think it has anything to do with him," she said urgently, giving Jo a glance to see if she would question her statement. Jo's face remained unchanging. "I think I just don't want to be involved with anyone in that way right now. Like, I don't want to keep searching for something that I'm not really even sure I want."

Jo ran her hand through her hair and then rested her chin on her propped-up arm on the bar. "That sounds like a pretty great place to be in." She smiled at Jo who responded with her own soft smirk.

"I just hate this part, especially when he's a nice guy. I have a feeling he's not the type who will just want to stay friends," she grumbled regretfully. She caught a sudden change in Jo's face and a sinking feeling hit her stomach. Jo was now staring through the wall behind the bar—her eyes looking at something in the distance—then seemingly through whatever it was.

She felt her cheeks warm with the physical feeling of guilt for not thinking about Jo before she spoke. A few months ago, she had watched Jo fall in love. She had stayed cautiously optimistic for Jo as she had never become involved in that way with another person. She had watched them connect with each other in the kind of way people hope for. The kind of connection people try so hard to get—the kind of connection people try to force and as a result usually go forever without.

Her cautious optimism for Jo and the man who had come into Jo's life stemmed from him being separated, yet still tethered. Jo had chewed her lip when telling her that he had been upfront about his pending divorce before their first date—but the date for the divorce finalization was set, and so Jo had stopped chewing her lip and let herself fall in love.

It brought her physical pain to remember the night Jo came to her a few weeks ago—disheveled and heartbroken. One of the children had been having a lot of problems and it was realized that most of them stemmed from the separation and anticipated divorce. Jo had told her how he had just kept apologizing repeatedly with tears in his eyes, saying he had to go back—he had to go back for his children.

"How are you doing?" she asked Jo softly, who started slightly and broke her gaze from the world behind the wall. Jo's eyes had left the wall, but her mind hadn't completely come back with them.

"It doesn't seem to make sense—how relationships can just end," Jo murmured to her cup. "I guess it makes more sense when it happens over time—when it's a matter of people changing and growing apart. But how do people go from seeing each other every day, sharing the littlest things and the biggest things with each other to just nothing? Never seeing each other—never hearing each other. How did we go from wanting to hold each other and be with each other in every way possible, to not being part of each other's lives?" A hint of anger colored Jo's words.

"How can that make any sense if it was all real—if it was all true? How can I have been someone he loved one day and the next day someone he can just

21

go without?" Jo's hand on the bar clenched into a fist, but she could see the true hurt underneath Jo's anger. "What does that make me in his life? A mistake? A moment that came and went?" Jo seemed to sink into herself a little—shoulders dropping and spine bending with the weight of it all. "Are we really capable of just ending relationships like that? Moving on? Abandoning each other?" Jo's voice dropped back down to a whisper. "Abandoning me?"

She didn't know what to say. It was a moment in which there really was nothing to say. Her hand reached out and gently touched Jo's shoulder. Words weren't needed. Jo looked up at her with a tearful smile.

"That got a little dramatic, huh?" Jo wiped her eyes and tried to laugh it off with an empty chuckle. She took her hand off of Jo's shoulder and shrugged her own.

"Just truthful to yourself," she replied softly and watched Jo's smile drop and head nod in agreement down at her cup. "It really does kind of seem inhuman—for us to be able to care so deeply about people and then be able to stop when we want to or need to." It was her turn to stare into her cup with a furrowed brow. Is that what it was—every time she broke up with someone or moved on from a friendship? Did she just abandon people even if it was mutual abandonment? Was it inhuman if it was constantly done from one human to the next? Or did that make it very much human?

She shook her head and felt the tension in her forehead ease. The drink from her cup filled her mouth and after she swallowed, she could still feel the slight pleasant burn. The smile on her face felt as though it resonated the kindness she felt within her as she looked back over at Jo.

"I don't think we necessarily stop caring. Maybe in some cases, but probably not in most. I think that we still care even in the absence of all the stuff that made us open ourselves up to caring in the first place." She took a hold of Jo's hand on the bar and held the clamminess of it in the warmth of hers. "And I don't think you can really abandon people if you still care about them—still love them—even if you can't be with them or show up for them the way you did before. I think that's how we're capable of ending relationships—by knowing they're not ours to have anymore, but still caring that they existed."

Jo's facial expression was soft with emotion before she raised her eyebrows and shook her head.

"Shit." Jo smirked and squeezed her hand. "You better write that down. I might need to hear that again someday."

She winked, returning Jo's smile. "Don't worry, I'll be around to tell you it on repeat whenever you need."

Both their cups lifted off the bar at the same time and with a dull *clink* and shared smiles both of them tossed back the rest of their drinks with a gulp.

"Alright, we've been talking about me and my shit way too much recently," Jo said with a shake of her head. "So what are you going to be doing with all of your free time now that you're swearing off men?"

The air seemed lighter with Jo's genuine smile playing upon her lips. In response to Jo's words, she rolled her eyes taking a turn to shake her own head.

"I'm not swearing off men. Geesh, you are in a dramatic mood." She paused trying to consider what her words had actually meant. Contradicting thoughts and feelings filled her—desire to be alone and fear of loneliness. "Maybe just no pressure companionship is what I'm aiming for."

"Companionship? Is that they're calling it now?" She shot Jo a glare.

"That's not what I—"

"I know, I know," Jo interrupted her protests. "I wouldn't be judging you though." She caught a slight shade of bitterness in Jo's voice that softened her again. "Are you planning on starting a new hobby or something? I'd say scrapbooking. I think you'd make a really good scrapbooker."

She playfully hit Jo on the shoulder—hard enough

to where Jo rocked slightly on her stool, laughing. She got up off her own stool and grabbed their empty cups off the bar—walking them around to the sink. The warm water ran over her hands as she looked around the shop—the thing that belonged to her, but didn't really belong to her.

What did belong to her? What existed in the world that was of her? Soap bubbles covered each of her fingers as squeezed the sponge out over the cups.

She knew she wanted partnership, family, kids to belong to her—someday. But even then, would they belong to her? Should they *belong* to her? She didn't think so. The cups made a gentle thud on the shelves as she set them down. Her hands were still lightly damp as she realized she had inadequately dried them, distracted by her thoughts.

Jo had stayed sitting at the bar—turned around to face the rest of the shop—taking in all the pieces, the experiences that belonged to the four walls.

"I'm probably going to start putting in some more hours, actually," she thought out loud, causing Jo to spin around with a quizzical look.

"Is that really what you're aiming for, just working more?" Jo asked incredulously.

"You know it's more than that for me. The amount of people I get to meet in one day—how much more companionship can I get?" She looked passed Jo and out the tall windows where she could catch glimpses of shadows walking by—every now and then enough light catching them so the shadows became people.

"I think I'm going to put in more hours for a while and then do a bit of traveling," she thought out loud. "Meet some different people, see some different things." She broke her gaze from outside the window and smiled down at her hands on the bar. "Let myself find some experiences to belong to."

Jo hit the bar in enthusiasm. "Sounds like a plan to me! You go out and see some of the world. And if you don't get to see it all, when you get back, I'll put you to work and go see the rest of it for you."

"Deal." She smiled, feeling as though something in her felt more settled and more excited all at the same time.

2003

"What's your recommendation? I'm a little lost."

She was jolted by his words. She hadn't even realized she was on autopilot—giving a greeting, taking an order, responding with a smile. She saw his eyes investigate the menu behind her head, seeking some kind of answer, and then come back to her face expectantly.

"Making you feel a little lost is part of the charm," she responded with slight sarcasm. Instantly, she grimaced as the words left her mouth feeling a twinge of embarrassment. If she had been more present, she never would have thought to say something like that to a new customer. His eyebrows lifted slightly and she saw the corner of his mouth twitch before breaking into a small smirk. Immediately the embarrassment fled. "A recent one we've come up with is a lavender sea salt mocha." His eyebrows shot up a little further, looking more questioning than affronted.

27

"Lavender. Really? That's pretty different. Another part of the charm?" He pursed his lips together in consideration as the smirk still lay upon his lips. Her autopilot smile was replaced by a genuine one as she watched the intrigue in his eyes.

"We've got charm all over the place."

A full-on grin broke through his face, and she noticed a slight twinkle of amusement in his eyes. At one point in her life, she would have maybe considered her interaction with him flirting. She wasn't sure what had changed over the last year or so, but she stopped seeing such interactions as flirtatious. Flirting entailed a certain effort to make oneself seem attractive. She had started to see interactions like this attractive in themselves, independent of the people involved. It made the exchange of words all day long with others seem more enjoyable, almost an art—creating a lasting impression through a single interaction.

"You convinced me. I'll take one."

Money was exchanged, hot liquids poured, milk frothed, the cup handed from hers to his. Moments of the day pushed forward. Her mind continued on its previous path, finding its way through as she carried on with her tasks, going back into autopilot.

His eyes excitedly scanned the offer for what felt like the millionth time. Negotiations had seemed to go as

*far as they were going to, and he was more than pleased
with what the final offer was. As he looked at the salary,
his stomach fluttered. He would probably never tell his
father how much he would be making—even just to start
he realized, and swallowed his excitement trying not
to let it show too much on his face. He wouldn't want
any injury to his father's pride, but at the same time, he
knew he'd be so proud of him. How often had he heard
his father say that money wasn't the most important
thing in life, but that if he was able to work hard to get
to a point of not having to worry about it, it sure made
life easier? His chest tightened with emotion as he knew
full well that it was a luxury to have the opportunity to
receive such an offer—a luxury given to him through
the work of the man he was just thinking of.*

*"Thanks, Dad," he whispered softly as he scribbled his
signature and carefully slid the paperwork back into
the large envelope.*

*He felt himself exhale—not realizing he had been
holding his breath and leaned back into the soft chair.
Grabbing the cup—still warm but no longer steaming—he brought it to his lips and sipped the liquid
enjoying the immediate flavors that hit his tongue. The
bitterness of the coffee seemed to be folded gently into
the subtle sweetness of the chocolate and smooth cream,
and touched with the sharp flavor of sea salt all held in
the light earthy sweet taste of lavender. Immediately
he refilled his mouth with more than a sip and found*

himself surprised at how enjoyable the drink was.

His eyes scanned the coffee shop with all of its pleasing aesthetic and innate warmth. Maybe this could be a new regular place, so close to his soon-to-be office. The table next to him held a couple of books, the top one a seemingly old travel book. He relaxed into the comfort of the chair thumbing through the pages, not truly paying attention but enjoying not having to.

As he took another sip he looked up and saw the woman who was at the counter flitting around among some of the tables on the other side of the room—grabbing a cup here and there, exchanging some words and then a laugh or two with those sitting enjoying their drinks. Her movements could not be considered graceful, but the way she moved was with a kind of ease that seemed to flow to the people around her, as though the movements and interactions they created were something so familiar to her body they were just as natural as breathing.

During the half-hour he spent finishing his drink and looking through different books, his thoughts didn't include the woman; however, he found the awareness of her stayed with him.

* * *

A flutter made itself known in the pit of her stomach, slight, but enough for her to be aware of it. She internally rolled her eyes at herself. But he was attractive—his laugh was rich which was what had made the sudden flutter occur. Was something different about him today? Maybe he had done something with his hair? Or had she just not noticed over the past few weeks he had been coming in? She noticed now.

He noticed a subtle shift in her demeanor. It was almost as though she became self-conscious for the first time since he had met her. It wasn't a lack of confidence, but a sudden awareness and thoughtfulness of herself. It brought him a small amount of comfort, for it was a feeling he had been experiencing since the second time he'd seen her. She looked down at her hands and then back up at him with a look that made his heart jump.

"Seems like you might actually have the best part of the deal—getting out of the office for a break. Being the coffee boy might not be such a bad thing." She wiped the deep wood counter and kept her hands busy arranging things, trying to ignore him looking at her. Not that it wasn't nice for him to be looking at her, but she was wishing she hadn't noticed how attractive he was. She wished she could just see the same face she had been getting used to—just another friendly visitor she saw every day.

"I'm thinking it's not a bad thing at all." His voice was a little softer, but residue from his laughter still clung to his words. She quickly turned away to hide the blush that rose on her cheeks, silently cursing her body for such a reaction.

He slid off the barstool and found himself regretfully taking the tray of cups from her, not ready to say goodbye for the day. The look she had given him had hooked him with intrigue, making him wonder if she would look at him like that again. With the unsteady weight of multiple sloshing cups, his focus was instinctually shifted to the task at hand. He smiled at her and was lifted by the one she gave him in return.

"See you—see you tomorrow," he stammered as he realized the way he had grabbed the cup trays was not making leaving any easier. Her response was light and once more carefree with a slight motion from two of her fingers—a quirky wave and salute that was her standard farewell. His response felt like an awkward nod as he backed through the door, mentally patting himself on the back for having turned his coworkers on to the coffee shop. They were all so appreciative of his willingness to take on the daily mid-morning coffee run.

* * *

32

The soft thud of the door made her shift from leaning forward on the counter to a more upright position as, Ashley—an employee—gave her a wave while hustling through the door as if indicating her entrance should be ignored.

"I forgot my coat. I'm just running to the back to get it," Ashely explained breathlessly, not taking any time to stop.

Looking out the window it had surprised her how dark it had gotten over the last hour. Ashley rushed back through the shop, gave a wave and a "see you later" before the door thudded once more.

"Do you want a little fill-up?" She nodded towards the cup snug between his hands that was only a quarter full at this point.

"No, thanks. I feel like I've become progressively over-caffeinated recently." He smiled at her and lifted an accusing eyebrow.

"I don't know why you're looking at me like that, I'm not spiking your drinks with extra espresso or anything." She leaned back down so her elbows and forearms rested on the counter across from him. A slight groan escaped as she felt her back stretch. She proceeded to bend her neck feeling the full flex of the muscle. A sound of amusement made her glance up. "What?"

"Wasn't expecting you to have a full-on cat moment, that's all." She rolled her eyes at him.

"Must be nice just sitting around all day in your little office chair, rolling yourself around everywhere."

"Is that what working in an office is like? Really? Just a bunch of us rolling around in our chairs from office to office, playing bumper cars in the halls?" She felt the snort come through her nose trying to keep the liquid she just drank in her mouth and not spewed onto his face. He gave a devilish smirk as he watched her comedic struggle, tapping his finger on his chin feigning a pensive look at the ceiling. "Actually, that would be a good leg work out. Makes sense why everyone at my office has such jacked legs."

Her laughter was brought forward by him giving into his own. She liked laughing with him.

He took a breath trying to calm his laughter as hers subsided and she shook her head at him, taking another drink from her cup. He followed suit and drained the last bit of liquid from his own. A comfortable silence followed their laughter. Faint music played over the speakers, but other than that, there was just comfortable silence.

Often around this time of night, he was the only customer. Most people probably weren't looking to be caffeinated at six o' clock at night, he noted. Most people had headed home to decompress for the day or, if heading out anywhere, to a bar for a more physically depressing drink. For the last month, he'd been stopping by after leaving the office. At first, he came just to sit and relax somewhere cozier than his apartment, but often it was then just the two of them, or at least just her and another staff member.

The one-liners between them had slowly grown to conversations that lasted twenty to thirty minutes—often only interrupted by a stray customer who was in and out or one of the other employees noting how it was time for them to head home. He noticed how over the past two weeks once he got there, she would just tell whoever was still working to not worry about staying until close. This had resulted in a couple raised eyebrows and a "are you sure?" from a couple of employees at first, but now they gave him a smile and started gathering their stuff together when he came in.

He had noticed that due to the caffeine intake later at night he was having difficulty falling asleep before midnight. Despite the more difficult mornings, he found himself back at this counter across from her every night during the week.

A buzz from his phone broke the pillow of silence that she had been resting in. She grabbed his now empty cup and brought it over to the sink. A quick glance at her watch made her sigh a little with the recognition of another workday done. She wiped the counter and watched him flip open the phone, his eyes going from questioning to a grimace of surprise.

"That was a look!" she observed audibly. His grimace deepened as he fumbled to put his phone in his pocket and looked somewhat sheepishly at her, making her laugh a little. "What?"

"I have to get going, sorry, I know I usually help you with the chairs." He got up and ran his hand over his hair as he looked around the shop. "I just—I totally forgot I'm meeting someone for dinner." An initial feeling hit her at his words but was then so quickly swept aside by slight panic, that she didn't even have time to identify it.

"Wait, is it Thursday?!" She swiveled her head around looking for a calendar on a nearby wall that she knew didn't exist. His sheepish expression dropped, now showing interest at her quick behavior change and wide eyes.

"Yeah, it's Thurs—"

"Shit!" She hurriedly ran around the bar and started picking up chairs and putting them on tables. Out the corner of her eye, she saw him looking at her with wonderment. "I'm supposed to meet someone for drinks in two minutes," she growled, frustrated at herself for ending up in a position to be rushed.

Gratitude softened her as she saw him start

putting chairs on the tables with her, followed by sudden regret. "No, please, I'm fine. I don't want you to be late for your date." She felt herself getting sweaty at the sudden exertion and felt a jab of annoyance again. Just the vibe she wanted to bring on a date. She heard him mutter something to the effect of *don't worry about it.* She felt herself calm a little, glad he was there.

The last chair made a soft thud on the table as he let go of it and looked around the room finding her in front of one of the mirrors hanging on the wall—fidgeting with her hair now loose, running her finger under her eyes and gliding some lipstick over her lips.

The face of his date seemed to vanish from his mind. He couldn't even recall her having a face at the moment.

"Go, get out of here! There's no use in us both being late," she exclaimed, her hands flapping at him to go. She grabbed her coat and did something quick with the cash register to lock it. He noticed her boots, the black leather traveling over her ankles with a slight heel on the back. He imagined those heels hooked on to the bottom rung of a barstool pointed toward the legs of an unknown person. "I really appreciate your help. I'll just come in early to do some extra cleaning." He snapped himself out of it— whatever it was—and walked over to the door putting on his jacket as well.

"Yeah, no problem. I usually help, I felt bad leaving

you to do it all."

They both stopped in their mutual rush before the door unable to get out at the same time. She looked up at him and her hand gently touched his arm.

"Thank you again for helping." Her eyes. His date. He had a date. She had a date. He cleared his throat and her arm dropped.

"Enjoy your drinks."

"Enjoy your dinner."

He pushed open the door and walked away to his date with the woman whose face he couldn't remember.

* * *

Christmas music played lightly throughout the shop with some notes of jazz weaving in and out of the melody. The foundational smell of the coffee shop always stayed the same but around the holidays hints of cinnamon, nutmeg and peppermint wafted about, seducing customers to try a seasonal drink. Swift movements caught her eye as she finished placing a cleaned cup on the shelf. She turned to see him dancing with the mop, twirling it around with surprising finesse then looking over, seeing if he caught her eye. A broad grin appeared on his face when he saw that he had. She felt a similar smile reflect across her lips and shook her head playfully.

"That's probably the first dance that girl's had. Careful she may just fall in love with you."

"Ha, with my charm and good looks she's already in love."

A brief snort came from her throat toward him as she finished putting the last of the cups on the shelf. She found herself smiling feeling a warmth inside that she'd become accustomed to during their closing time together.

As he finished gliding the mop across the floor, he found himself glancing up at her. He wasn't even conscious of it at first, but then became self-conscious and found himself having to make an effort not to look at her. Her hands moved swiftly but in a relaxed way as she cleaned the different machines behind the counter. Even though he was across the room, he could see her mouth the words to a song that had started playing at some point. There was a subtle sway in her hips and suddenly he was very much aware of her body.

This awareness was not new to him, but he often tried to not indulge in it. But he was finding it difficult. The denim of her jeans hugged her legs and butt, ending at the small swoop of her lower back where every now and then a sliver of her skin would peek through under the edge of her shirt. He shook his head, trying to dislodge his thoughts, and walked back to the office where the supply cabinet was. He enjoyed what they had, would hate to make things uncomfortable by trying to make it more than it was. Shaking his head again he put the mop back and then ran his hand over his hair with an instinctual anxious twitch.

Her eyes searched for him. She found herself irked when she didn't see him. Where was he? Did he leave? Would he leave without saying goodbye? He'd never done that before.

The distant sound of the supply closet door closing brought her relief. He must have slipped back there to put the mop away when her back was turned. Her relief gave away to frustration at how silly her reaction had been. She felt silly. She didn't like feeling silly. This had started becoming a more recent occurrence—her feeling silly concerning him, specifically when he wasn't there in front of her face, sharing space with him, breathing the same air.

She would come across something and think of telling him, wondering if he would like it or find it interesting. Five o'clock would hit, and she would start glancing at the door.

A couple weeks ago he had gone out of town to visit family. The first night without him coming to the shop had been close to miserable, everything feeling mundane, and she had entered her apartment feeling wildly dissatisfied. She had ended up booking herself up the next handful of nights with friends and a date or two. The endgame of one of her dates had become quickly apparent and it startled her to find herself entangled on a couch with someone else, thinking about how he would taste. Her body pleasantly tensed with the recollection of it and, catching herself, she angrily pushed the register's drawer closed. Silly.

The lights behind the counter had already been flicked off and she was making her way to the door with her coat and bag, doing little finishing tasks as she went. He picked up his own coat from the leg of an upside-down chair and started toward the door as well.

"What days are you closed next week?" Her eyebrows furrowed into a question. "For Christmas," he clarified. Her eyebrows relaxed and she shrugged her shoulders.

"None. We have one staff who doesn't celebrate it as a holiday, another who doesn't have family around and likes to stay busy. Other than getting together with friends, I don't fly out to see my parents until the weekend after." She flicked another light switch so only the recess lighting for half the room was left on. "We just do shortened hours and whoever is working can close when they want based on how many people come in. Sometimes people need a place to go. Those of us who always have one can forget that." Her voice was

41

soft at her last statement, and he didn't pick up any kind of bristling or accusation. She flicked off the last switch so all that was left on were a couple of security lights in the back and the string lights hanging outside.

"I get that." His own voice matched her softness as he looked down at his shoes which had seemed to disappear into the darkness of the shadows flooding the floor. Loneliness was not new to him. Moving farther than he ever had from the neighborhood he grew up in was harder than he thought it was going to be. He hadn't known what to do with himself, where he belonged outside of work and his apartment—not until he had walked through the door he was now standing next to, and the voice he was now so familiar with told him that making him feel lost was part of the charm.

His eyes slowly drifted up through the darkness to where her hand hung by her leg. Just hanging there loose and empty. Light from the string lights outside seemed to glint off her dark painted nails. He didn't think, but rather just watched his hand reach out to hers feeling the warmth of her fingers being held in between his. Her fingers were solid and soft, light and heavy, all at the same time. His eyes met hers and that's all he saw. Just her eyes—her eyes seeing him.

He must have taken a step because he found himself closer to her. Shadows covered half her face, but not deep enough where he couldn't see her lips slightly parted, a subtle flush on the lighted cheek, and both her eyes

42

gleaming at him. Her fingertip twitched and the spell was broken—his hand dropping hers in surprise.

A sinking feeling as she had never known broke throughout her entire body as he dropped her hand and turned toward the door. She had felt it—it was palpable—the energy between them, coming from them, one to the other. She wanted him. With the drop of her hand, she felt everything else within her drop, her eyes following the downward pull felt throughout her entire body. He had stopped it. He had chosen to stop it and now he was walking away—

The hand on her cheek pulled her face upward as she felt the other hand and arm wrap around her body pulling her up against him, his body solid and warm. Her arms flung themselves around his shoulders and one of her hands instinctually went up to his neck and burrowed in his hair. Their tongues wrapped around each other in the shared space their mouths created. Everything was soft and firm at the same time. He held her tighter, and she felt her whole body subtly shudder and give in to him. Her mind was blank. There was no emotion. There wasn't room for any—no space for anything other than the moment between them.

When their mouths separated, he noticed the feeling of

43

electricity throughout his entire body and thought his muscles actually had a slight shake to them. He peered down into her eyes and guided a strand of hair behind her ear with the tip of his finger, enjoying the softness of her cheek when doing so.

"I've wanted to do that for a long time," he whispered huskily. Her eyes smiled into his.

"Me too."

04/16/2005

A burning sensation climbed up his nose as the wine caught in the back of his throat while he tried to stifle a laugh, and keep his mouthful of wine, from exiting. He felt the attempt backfire as the wine tried to find a way out through his nasal passages instead. Somehow, he caught his breath and regained his faculties, keeping the wine in his mouth and then coaxing it down his throat where it belonged.

"Are you trying to kill me? Saying something like that while my mouth is full!" He shook his head in mock chastising as she gave him a devilish smile.

"What? You know it's true. That's exactly what he looks like. If you deny it then you're just lying to yourself." She gave a dramatic sigh and took a sip from her own glass, crossing her legs which were between his—her feet reaching just above his knee under the blanket.

"I'm never going to be able to go into his office without thinking that now." He shook his head

and took another sip of wine—this one successfully making its way down his throat without any
trouble. His eyes drifted over to the edge of the
roof about two yards from where they sat on
the oversized wicker couch. There weren't many
buildings in the direction he was looking higher
than theirs, and if he kept his eyes level, it felt as
though it was just them and the sky. Stars could be
seen faintly over and beyond them—gleaming specs
that could be discerned with enough concentration.
Even though it was late at night, the sky was a navy
blue color instead of the pure black that occurred
when untampered by the lights of streets and
buildings. He found himself comfortably voicing
his thoughts out loud as he looked into the vastness
above them.

"Do you remember the house in the mountains
we stayed at? How bright the stars were? I don't
think I've ever seen anything like it." Her feet
shifted gently against his legs as she followed his
gaze.

"Yeah, nothing like we've ever seen here. It was
pretty amazing," she whispered softly, her voice
then changing in tone. "The hot tub made it seem
even better. How hard do you think it would
be to get a hot tub up here? Do you think the
building manager would mind?" The sky released
his gaze and he shook his head at her looking

46

around jokingly as if scouting out the best place for a hot tub.

"He doesn't seem to mind a couch up here, so a hot tub isn't too much to ask," he shrugged sarcastically and squeezed her feet with his knees. He was sure that their little rooftop getaway was not as much of a secret as they liked to pretend it was. The first time she had led him up the maintenance stairs—rolling her eyes and grabbing his hand as he protested—they had both looked around in amazement at the view. There wasn't much on the roof except for the wicker couch they were sitting on now, upside down near a concrete structure which was most likely part of the ventilation system. The couch had needed to be wiped off after an unknown amount of time without use, and they had brought up a few old couch cushions that were then kept inside the door to the roof. It had become their special spot when they didn't want to go out, but the apartment was feeling a little too confining.

He smiled to himself as his thumb stroked the smooth surface of the wine glass. There had been one occasion when he was walking down the stairs back to their apartment to grab the pizza they had cooking in the oven—he had frozen as one of the building management employees came out of the supply closet in the middle of the hallway.

The older man had looked at him in surprise, eyes quickly assessing the two empty beer bottles in his hand along with her jacket that she had decided she hadn't really needed. He gave the man a sheepish smile of guilt—one that he was sure his parents had seen a handful of times when he was a teenager. The older man's mouth twitched and then in one swift motion he rolled eyes, waved his hand in a nonchalant dismissive way, and turned down the hallway disappearing around the corner.

He had never told her about the incident. He knew part of the charm for her was the idea that no one else knew they went up there.

"Actually, maybe we shouldn't push our luck." She gave a dramatic sigh at his statement while reaching down to grab a chip from the bag resting against the leg of the couch. He watched her contently gaze beyond the roofline as the chip was consumed with a satisfying crunch. He looked back up at the sky and then back down to her.

Should he bring it up? It wasn't as though he were going to try and get her to make a decision tonight. She seemed in a good enough mood. "We could have a hot tub. In a yard somewhere. Belonging to a house. Our house. Our house somewhere where the sky gets dark enough so we could see the stars."

Her head snapped back to look at him, but her facial expression didn't seem to carry any annoyance or frustration. He felt himself relax as the sense of caution ebbed away.

"Hm." Her eyes looked him up and down in an accusatory sort of way. "I guess I set myself up for that one, didn't I?" He smiled and grabbed at one of her big toes, playfully squeezing it between his fingers.

"I'm just trying to make your hot tub dreams come true."

She made a little half-bow with her head and shoulders while rolling her eyes, her voice dripping with sarcasm, "I'm so grateful for your selflessness, my husband dear." Her foot gave a slight kick dislodging her toe from his grasp.

"All for you, my dearest wife," he shot back with a smile saturated in sweetness. The corner of her pursed lips lifted to a smirk, and she threw a chip at him, which he fumbled with for a minute before crunching down on it in victory.

"It's irritating how cute you are sometimes," she said through a soft smile. It was the kind of smile that still made his stomach jump. She then looked down at the glass in her hands and he noticed how her face had changed when looking back up at him. She looked more reserved—somewhat pensive and doubtful. "I think it's ironic to want something so bad and then, when it's available, what you currently have is too perfect to mess with." Her eyes went back down to the glass. "Sometimes I feel stuck, but happy to be stuck where I am. It's confusing."

He smiled at her, trying to show understanding while not quite having it. She was not often a person he would describe as vulnerable—but in the rare moments she was he tried to make sure she knew it was safe to be. "You're one of the most confident and able people I know," he said assuredly. Her responding look was one he couldn't read.

"Do you know how terrifying that can be" she whispered, "to be seen as someone who is always confident and able? What if there are times I'm not? Does that mean I'm not who I used to be? Does that mean I never was who people thought I was? It's a lot of pressure. Another piece of irony—confidence being broken down by having lack of confidence in having continued confidence." She made a soft snort and took a sip of wine. He was listening and trying to understand, but at the same time he knew he could probably never fully understand what she was trying to come to terms with. He was just a close spectator. He had realized that when she was in her thoughts that's all he could be—usually all she wanted him to be—a living soundboard.

He wasn't sure what his facial expression was, but when she looked back at him the soft smile was back. It gave him a sense of relief. The rabbit hole hadn't been too deep or at least she hadn't gone down it too far.

"I'm just feeling much more confident in what we have going on now than the possibilities of the future. It's like my papa used to say, it's not a no, not a yes, just not now."

He returned her soft smile and rubbed her feet which had found their way back to his hands again. Her statement brought understanding and relatability. He was excited about the idea of finding a house, of growing their family the way they had generally talked about. Fear and doubt crept in at times too though. He could fill his entire head of anxiety-tainted "what ifs" if he let himself, but then he would look at her, and a different kind of "what if" would fill his head—one filled with hopes and dreams.

"I know." His fingers gently pressed on the bottom of her blanketed foot which instinctually squirmed a little as he touched a certain pressure point. She was perfect right where she was—with him and the sky. His shrug seemed to lighten the air.

"I was just talking about getting a hot tub," he said through a smirk. As another chip flew through the air, her laughter came along with it—both softly falling against his face in unison.

The night air seemed to relax his lungs as he took

51

deep breaths, and he felt his mind start drifting across the night sky. He felt completely content right here with her. The feeling was reminiscent of the many nights they spent together sitting in the warm coffee shop, enjoying the simplicity of friendship.

Then he was taken back to lying in her bed for the first time—her body folded into his. Her hair was soft against his lips and chin, his hand cupped underneath her butt, her soft skin pressed against his pelvis. They had laid there, every now and then exchanging a thought, but then in the silence he would be able to feel and listen to her breathing.

The stars drifted with him to the kitchen in their apartment filled with the warm smells of cooking food as they whirled around each other, each taking care of their own dish for a shared meal. Laughter mixed with the music playing in the background. She had straightened up from putting a dish in the oven, a strand of hair loose in her face. With the tip of his finger, he had guided it back behind her ear, his palm caressing her cheek, warm from the heat of the oven. They stood there for a moment, close but not completely touching. The smell of spices wafted in the air around them.

The stars brought back the thumping of music in his chest as they clung to each other's fingers and spun around together at his sister's wedding.

Just aware enough of the others on the dance floor to avoid knocking anyone over. Remembering the sight of her neck and the neon lights from the DJ booth dancing upon it as she let her head fall back in childlike fashion, laughing so large he could see the back of her throat.

Looking up from his book and seeing her grinning next to him on their bed with her book propped up on her knees. "This is how it's going to be, isn't it?" she said making a slight nod to the books in their hands.

"This is the dream, isn't it? We just need reading glasses for full effect." She wrinkled her nose at him and then went back to her book.

"Just so domesticated," she stated primly. He looked over at her tied-up hair above her long neck. He could see her eyes darting around the page trying to find the spot she left off at. A slight thrill ran through his body as he shifted slowly.

"Domesticated, huh?" His voice was gruff as he suddenly threw his book to the side, quickly followed by hers and then rolled himself on top of her as she let out a shriek of laughter.

The feel of her toes wiggling on the inside of his knee brought his attention back from the stories being held by the stars. She let out a small yawn and then blinked her eyes at him questioningly.

"Are you ready to call it a night?"

He looked at her sitting across from him under the stars in the night air, adjusting the blanket over her stomach.

"I'm not saying no," he said softly. She looked up at him—the stars that were hidden in the lighted sky shining in her eyes. Her voice was barely above a whisper in response.

"But you're not saying yes."

"Just not now."

08/21/2005

I t took her brain a moment to register what she was seeing. The dark red blood had seeped throughout her entire underwear.

She hadn't felt anything. She hadn't felt the uncomfortable oozing of fluid. It had just been there when she pulled down her pants and sat on the toilet—the metallic smell suddenly letting itself be known and the blood-drenched underwear staring up at her. For a split second, she felt a sense of horror at the possibility that the blood had leaked through her pants onto the couch, but after a quick check of the outside crotch area of her pants she ruled that out as a possibility.

Robotically, she wiped herself and felt mildly surprised to see the bright red blood shining vividly on the white toilet paper. She felt her heart start beating faster as she looked down at the dark clot in the middle of it all—almost black if not examined closely. Her hand dropped the saturated paper into the toilet bowl underneath her. She continued to wipe without much thought, but with a sense of urgency trying to understand what she was experiencing—what was happening to her body.

The test was in the garbage next to her, wrapped in toilet paper, and stuffed down into the can in case he had suddenly become interested in investigating the garbage. It sat there next to her, wrapped and covered in its own world of trash silently emitting a faint message with a bold line displayed through the plastic window next to another line much, much fainter—but there.

She was going to tell him. She had just wanted to wait—wait a couple days to see if the line would grow in boldness, in surety. She was going to tell him.

She realized she had frozen staring at another deep blackish-red blob the size of a nickel. It hit her. The line wouldn't be growing in boldness. There wouldn't be any surety. Or maybe there would be—of a different kind. She couldn't comprehend it all. Her heart was heavy with disappointment as she felt the broken hope of possibility—the possibility of the baby that would have come to be. Who would it have been? Would the possibility have grown into their son, or would it have been their daughter? Tears sprung up in her eyes, light enough that they didn't yet fall.

Then there was the fear. A fear she had never

felt before because it was a thought she had never thought before: *what if I'm not able?*

Not once had the thought come to her before. There had never been doubt. A sharp stab of shame hit her. She felt the body that encased her—that belonged to her—and felt shame. Why hadn't it done what it was supposed to?

She folded the paper, squishing the clot before letting it fall into the water. Should she tell him? What would he think? How would he feel? How would he feel about her?

Her brain told her she was wrong to even question him having a supportive reaction, but the fear and shame whispered.

She wouldn't tell him. She'd never kept something from him. But she couldn't tell.

She'd protect him—there wasn't any need for him to experience any disappointment or anxiety.

She felt nauseous. Standing up, she finished cleaning herself—the rag she wetted in the sink cold and rough against her stained inner thighs. She felt very aware of her own body. Most of all, she felt betrayed by it.

II

Summer

07/10/2006

"Ah! Damnit, get out of here!"

She resisted opening her eyes for a minute at the sound of his voice. When reluctantly cracking her eyes open, she saw the sky above tinged a deceptive golden brown by the lens of her sunglasses. A wisp of white passed through her vision as a solitary cloud slid across the sky.

Everything was comfortably warm. The sunshine caressed her legs lying on the soft sand, pressed down by the weight of her body and forming a natural bed around her thighs and calves. She was aware of the weight of her own hand on her stomach as she breathed slowly. Covering her fingertips were small grains of sand creating a rough texture on her smooth skin. The soft swish of water hitting the shore was barely noticeable unless consciously paid attention to. The sound was so constant that it had just become part of existence in the moment.

"That was close." His voice broke through the

silence that wasn't silent.

She turned her head and looked over as he sat down next to her—his forearm filled her field of vision. Light brown hair covered his skin. She could see flecks of sand that had either been captured by the hair or had leeched onto him to be carried to an unknown location—either another part of the beach or something as mundane as the car floormat. She wondered if maybe those specific grains would make it all the way home with them.

What kind of car ride would the sand witness? Would it be one starting with light-hearted conversation making its way to a topic that would become more somber and intense? Would it be a car ride filled with music that would have the random accompaniment of their voices on certain lines they knew or a chorus that pulled them out of their silence? Or would it be a ride where there was just silence, with neither one of them wanting to say anything or putting on music, for to do so would indicate that being together in silence was uncomfortable? Which kind of car ride would the grains of sand be witness to?

It seemed to her that the tone of car rides these days was always an uncertainty. She supposed uncertainty was natural with two humans trapped together while moving sixty miles per hour.

"Did you see that seagull? It started walking away

with the whole bag of chips. I guess it was too heavy for it to fly off with," he exclaimed with a sense of success at saving their snacks.

The rest of his torso moved slowly downward as he lowered himself to lie next to her, now looking at the same sky she was looking at moments ago. As she looked back at the sky, she realized it wasn't the same anymore—the wisp of cloud had moved on.

"I could lay here all day." He sighed and closed his eyes, folding his arms behind his head. She could tell by the soft smile on his lips that he believed what he said.

"No, you couldn't. I give you fifteen minutes before you're up again. It's not in your nature to lie anywhere all day."

His right eye popped open at her, and a smirk appeared across his lips, disregarding any frustration that she may have accidentally let season her words. "A man can try, can't he? Maybe I'll surprise you and make it seventeen minutes."

His lighthearted nature was contagious enough, and she felt herself smile along with him before sitting up.

The water was a grayish blue color today with white specks making their appearance when a wave big enough would roll onto the shore.

There weren't many people there with them—not

that they were with them. Or maybe they were. Maybe being in the same physical space as someone, automatically meant you were with them, and they were with you.

Two young girls played in the sand closer to the shore, filling buckets of water and then carrying them back to a sand-crafted masterpiece—their little bodies stiffening and curving at the weight of the water in their buckets. A hatted woman sat on a towel nearby, her eyes traveling from her book to the girls, to the water, to a teenage couple nearby, back to the girls, and then finally back to her book. Every now and then she would offer guidance or shoot unsolicited directions at the girls.

The teenage couple was further from the shore and, on second glance, realized she couldn't exactly tell if they were in fact teenagers or in their early twenties. The young woman lay with her back to the sun as her partner straddled her legs and ran his fingers up her back, untying the top of her bikini to rub lotion, or more likely oil, on her already bronzed back. He covered his hands with whatever cream or liquid it was and began to rub the young woman's back. After a few minutes, he looked around quickly—sharing some resemblance to a meerkat—and slid his hands under the woman's body to fondle her breasts and then back up around her back and down her butt where his crotch now sat.

She removed her gaze from the couple as even from a distance she could see the thin fabric of the young man's shorts start to rise.

She found herself smiling as people do when they are hit with pleasant nostalgia. A couple years ago, she was a young woman on the same beach—which had been empty at the time—feeling the coarse texture of sand on her skin accompanied by the softness of his lips—then tongue. His eyes gleamed in delight at her when realizing what was about to happen. With his face buried in her chest, she rode him to the rhythm of the waves. It was like a goddamn romance novel. Until the horseflies started biting her ass and she realized there was sand in crevices she didn't even know she had.

She looked at him now, still lying down, but with his foot subtly tapping the air—indicating that he had been still for longer than felt natural. She didn't think they had changed much, or not externally at least. His toes were still his toes; his feet still his feet; his legs still his legs; his stomach still his stomach; his chest still his chest; his arms still his arms; his neck still his neck; his chin still his chin; his lips still his lips.

She was reminded of how they were a couple years ago when first exploring each other. After a couple months of having developed a strong intimacy of friendship, the physical intimacy had been intoxicating—and the intoxication addicting. It had been ironically unnerving to her when the intoxication had died down, but her interest had not.

History had demonstrated to her that she most enjoyed the mutual lusting in a new relationship and often found herself a little bored and confused when it died down. He had been different—they had been different. She was comfortable with him in a way she had never been with another partner. Even in times of discomfort there was a steadiness—a lack of doubt in the existence of *them*.

Her eyes looked back out to the waves gliding onto the sand. They were still beautiful without the thrill of the crash.

Her mind stopped there as she shifted herself over him and let her lips naturally nestle in-between his, with light pressure becoming firmer at his reciprocation. Her hand pressed extra warmth onto his chest as if joining the sunlight in its warming endeavor. It was a kiss of desire in the sense that there was no expectation of more to come, but desire to feel his comfort and join in the comfort wholly.

A smile was left on his lips as their mouths parted. His hand briefly squeezed hers as she returned to her back looking up at the deceptively golden-brown sky. She noticed his foot had stopped its subtle tap. As she closed her eyes her thought went to the car ride home and the music they would most likely sing to. The sunshine caressed her, and everything was comfortably, steadily warm.

04/24/2007

P ale sunlight shone through the window
making the bright white walls of the room
seem a little sleepier—a little calmer. A slight
movement in her belly made her look down at
the firm rounded skin that made up most of her
abdomen. She wasn't sure if she had felt the
movement with her hand resting on her belly first,
or if it was the internal nudge alerting that the tiny
life inside of her was awake.

The stretched skin was smooth beneath her
fingers, and she was relieved to find that the itching
had subsided for the moment. She knew the
belly was hers, but it still gave her the strangest
sensation looking at it— something so abnormal
and unexpected in the most expected way. It was
hers but transformed by someone else—someone
else who was very much a part of her, who belonged
to her in one of the only ways a person could purely
belong to another.

At times, it didn't feel real when she looked down

at the vessel her body had become. She knew a tiny person was existing within, living a life, and having an experience different from her own. And yet, the little movements and, sometimes not so gentle prods from inside, reminded her that it was real. She leaned her head back on the rocker and noticed that the slight movement of her foot had been keeping her lightly rocking since sitting down.

The nursery was done, and she was sitting in the chair that she would be sitting in a month from now with her baby in her arms. She smiled to herself as she thought back to earlier at the coffee shop when Jo had pulled her aside.

She had not been smiling then, as she was getting incredibly tired of hearing her coworkers express concern for her doing tasks her body was completely used to. She had glared at Jo who had gently pulled her from behind the bar and back into the tiny hallway where the supply closet and office were.

"I'm fine. How many times do you need to hear me say it to believe me?" she snapped at Jo, feeling incredibly prickly and frustrated at how people were deeming her incapable of doing anything. She had pushed away the thought that her feet were killing her and the awareness of a possible muscle spasm blooming in her back.

69

Jo rolled her eyes at her and crossed her arms in front of her chest.

"Why would you think I would waste my time telling you something you already know?" Jo stated, eyes challenging her to say something contradictory.

She felt how hot her face was and hoped the sweat hanging above her upper lip was not too visible. Her body was a constant furnace now and any movement immediately made her break out in sweat.

"I'm going to tell you the truth because I know you won't sue me," said Jo sternly. "We're not worried about you spontaneously going into labor or wearing yourself down—although those would be very reasonable concerns." She heard herself give a very audible huff in response, which made Jo's eyebrow rise and mouth give a slight twitch. "The truth is that you and your big baby belly are slow and large and getting in the way. And no one wants to bump the pregnant lady or tell her to hurry up, but the truth is we all really do."

She felt speechless at first, not really knowing if she should start shouting or laughing. Jo's confident expression and crossed-arm stance stayed solid even though she could detect a slight nervousness in Jo's energy. Any frustration that was ready to pounce into anger gently subsided as she thought about how many times a day she was almost knocking into things behind the bar, including the coworkers who she thought were pitying her. A smile broke through her face as she realized they may have in fact been pitying themselves as they tried to maneuver around her with breakable cups full of hot liquid.

"Fine," she stated with a mocked seriousness. "If you are all struggling to work well because of me growing a child, then I guess I can stop coming in as much." Jo's eyebrow went up a notch.

"Okay," she sighed, and rolled her eyes as Jo gave a somewhat smug smile. "I'll start my maternity leave now, I guess."

A surprising amount of relief filled her when acknowledging how tired she was and how the long drive was becoming longer the more the baby grew. To add to the humor and annoyance of it all, the coworkers and customers who were in the shop at the time, all applauded when the commencement of her maternity leave was dramatically announced. Jo had reassured her before she left that they would expect visits after the baby was born and that a pack n' play would be set up in the office for when she wanted to start working again. They had both been excited about the plan, and the idea that the baby would grow up in the coffee shop the two of them had birthed together.

She caught herself about to start dozing and lifted her head up to look around the room. She had spent the rest of the day getting little things organized feeling as though everything was a little excessive, but then also wondering if they really had enough stuffed animals and if the baby would want more. It had turned out different than expected, but perfect, nonetheless.

Her gaze drifted out the window where she could faintly see the top of the tree in their backyard—its vibrant green leaves and pink blossoms bright against the clouds passing through the blue sky. She had never felt the need to have a big backyard or a lot of outdoor space, but when they had started looking at houses, she told him they at least needed one tree.

"I want to have a tree to sit under—for our kids to sit under. A tree that they can learn from," she had thought out loud, feeling herself get lost in thought while looking down at the list they were creating for what they wanted in a house.

He had cleared his throat to bring her attention back and looked at her—eyebrow raised. "Oh? Learn from?" A smile stayed constant on her face as she shared with him stories of sitting on her papa's porch at her grandparent's ranch when she was a little girl, and Papa telling her about the lessons of the trees.

Her hands gently rubbed a spot under the soft skin of her stomach that seemed a bit firmer than the rest. She wondered if the baby felt comforted as she rubbed the back or leg or head that pressed outward from inside.

"I think you're going to like your room." Her voice was soft and low as she spoke to the baby inside—hands caressing the belly as though it wasn't her own skin that felt the touch, but the skin of her little girl. "Your daddy was very proud of how we put everything together. He worked really hard to make sure everything you need would fit." A soft push near her pelvis warmed her entire body as the baby seemed to react to her voice. The skin of her stomach subtly shifted, and she could feel a larger area of firmness move underneath her fingers. A small part of her was sad at the thought of actually holding the baby in her arms soon—how was it going to be not holding the baby as close as she was now?

"Your daddy is so excited to meet you. I feel like I already know you, even though I have no idea what color hair you'll have or the shape of your face. I've felt you for the past eight months, baby girl, and I don't know if there's any more I need to know to truly know you." The room itself was silent with a gentle hum from the quiet neighborhood wafting in from the open window—quiet enough that the sound seemed to be caught in the arms of the nursery and soothed into silence. She found words flowing out of her comfortably and quietly as if the room brought such things forth.

"I don't know what kind of mom I'm going to be. I don't really know if there are different kinds of moms." As her voice got quieter and lower, she could feel the vibrations in her chest. "I can't wait to show you everything. There's so much to see, baby girl." Light tears sprung up in her eyes as she felt her entire being fill with emotion. "I hope I'll be a good mom for you. I hope I'll give you what you need and make you feel safe in this world. I might not do everything right and I'll probably make mistakes." The weight of the baby and subtle internal pressure suddenly gave the feeling that she could in fact see the baby, curled up within—small and beautiful. "But I promise you, baby girl, through it all I will love you with everything I have."

She stayed seated in the nursery for an unknown amount of time, imagining how it would all be—breathing in with joy the future moments the nursery held—that life with her baby held. She breathed it all in and was filled with all the hope of what would be.

74

05/17/2007

A soft stillness surrounded them, reflected in the baby's sleeping face. He was taken aback by how still the baby's face was—it made him question if the small body resting on his arm was not that of a toy doll. That's what the baby looked like to him—a perfectly crafted baby doll, lifeless to the world except for those who held her in their arms and loved her with all their heart. The tip of his finger gently stroked the cheek—its softness and bounciness confirming that it wasn't made of plastic or rubber. The baby was real and everything he had hoped she'd be—and more.

He looked at the infant, perplexed, realizing that the tip of his finger was the size of her entire cheek. Everything about the baby was so small he couldn't imagine that their noses were both noses—their eyes both eyes—their lips both lips. She was a human just as much as he was, even though she seemed wonderfully inhuman.

A soft snore from the hospital bed next to him

caused his attention to drift away from the baby.

She lay on the bed with the top slightly inclined—finally in a deep enough sleep to where she had stayed slumbering even after her head rolled to the side. Her mouth hung open slightly and a small string of drool was making its journey out of her mouth and onto the pillow. The blood vessels on her right cheek showed through her skin as though someone had drawn a map of purple and red riverbeds on her face. Looking over her tired form, his mind went back to the birth a few hours ago.

The adrenaline that had been rushing through his body made it impossible for him to identify what exactly he had been feeling—watching her face turn a color he had never seen before as she had pushed again at the direction of the doctor. He had been riding on waves of excitement, concern, and anxiety. Her eyes had gone bloodshot as she opened them long enough for him to see them before shutting her eyelids again with intensity. His entire body felt as though it were shaking from energy rather than weakness. The plastic railing on the side of the bed was under assault as her hand gripped it with a ferociousness next to his hands—also gripping the plastic to the point of knuckles turning white.

At one point she had demanded he not touch her anymore and had shaken his hand off hers while pushing air furiously through her mouth. Now his hands were only grabbing on for dear life.

His head had snapped over to the doctor as one of the nurses made a note of her blood pressure being "not where we want it to be". The doctor had a hand on the bottom of her protruding belly while the other hand dove into her vagina for direct investigation. The doctor had then made a comment heard through buzzing ears. In contrast, her roaring response cut through the buzzing as he heard her very clearly.

"I'm not fucking getting cut open too! Not after all of this shit!" Her face once more contorted, an exclamation was made from one of the nurses, and he felt his arm pulled while being moved closer to the end of the bed where her legs were bent, framing—he realized with shock—a small patch of hair in the middle of her stretched vaginal opening. His eyes stayed locked, watching one of the nurses bring a hand of the laboring body down to feel what was right there between its legs, ready to come out.

In hindsight, he wished he had been a little more conscious of his facial expression just in case she had caught a glimpse of it. However—also in hindsight—he was sure she was not paying much attention to him at that point.

His jaw had been clenched so tightly his teeth hurt afterward—his eyebrows furrowed with tension as he watched the opening of her vagina continue to spread and then move outward from her pelvis forming a short, thick exit tube.

He knew what he was seeing—at the same time he couldn't comprehend what he was seeing. Part of him needed to look away—part of him couldn't.

Her body just kept growing and opening—growing and opening. Words from the doctor and the nurses floated around him, but the only clear thing he could hear was her breathing and then grunts that would crescendo into yells. He heard them—he felt them.

As her body relaxed for a moment at the encouragement of a nurse, he stayed looking at what was very clearly the top of a head, covered in strands of dark hair mixed with slime and white coating. In a second of delirium, he almost laughed out loud as he realized the image in front of him was reminiscent of what it looks like when someone gets their head stuck in the tight neck of a turtleneck sweater. The laughter was quickly drowned by a wave of nausea as he realized that in this case the turtleneck sweater was made of out of skin and muscle—*her* skin and muscles—being stretched—and opened—a head trying to come out of it.

He was able to find enough control over his body to gently press his lips on the top of her calf. Her skin had the faint taste of salt, and a musty, yet somewhat chemical scent with the hint of defecation wafted up his nose. Then he was standing straight up again, and her body tensed—the yells breaking through the air.

The doctor's gloved hand cupped the bottom of the tubular opening while the other hand rested lightly on the protruding head. Her yell reverberated through his body as the top of the head slid the rest of the way through the opening, which widened slightly further with the exit of the baby's cheeks—the exit tube then retracting suddenly as pinkish red liquid spilled out behind the neck.

He let out a grunt of amazement and looked over at her head, now lying back on the pillow for another second of rest. He wanted to make sure she knew what had just happened—knew the amazing thing that just came out of her body. A smile had broken open on his face, but then slightly dimmed at the doctor's voice as he realized the rest of the body still had to come out too.

The skin of her arm was cool now as he reached out and laid his hand on her. She had amazed him—her body had amazed and terrified him—their new baby in his arms amazed him. Carefully, without

79

unsettling the tiny sleeping body on his other arm, he leaned over and kissed the skin right above the inside of her elbow. A light snore escaped her in response, as he let his lips rest on her skin for one more second—his back and neck awkwardly stretched.

"I love you so much," he whispered against her skin, feeling the air from his own words warm against his lips. "Thank you. Thank you for giving me her—for giving me you—thank you for letting me be a part of it all."

The tightness of the blood pressure cuff released slowly, the nurse gave a little nod of approval, and then rattled some numbers off that didn't have much meaning to her.

"Alright, I'm going to let you all rest for a little bit, and I'll be back in an hour to check on little girl and we'll see if she's ready to eat a little more, okay?" The nurse's voice was soft and kind as she gathered up the different supplies she had used to check her with. Her body felt so tired, yet her mind felt awake—though calm. She looked over at the hospital recliner where he had finally passed out reluctantly. He hadn't wanted to put the baby down even with the rolling bassinet right next to him.

From the bed, she could see the outline of the baby's

small body through the clear plastic—so small that if she hadn't been looking for the baby her eyes could have missed her. A sudden urge grabbed her, and she turned to the nurse somewhat timidly.

"Can I hold her for little bit? Is that okay?" The nurse's hand landed on her shoulder with a firm comforting grip.

"Of course, sweetie. I just want to make sure at some point you get a little bit of sleep, but you only get these kinds of moments once." The nurse had started moving as she talked, going over to the bassinet, and lifting the little body without any hesitation and then setting the baby down on her chest. "Would you like to do some skin-to-skin?"

She didn't know what she wanted. She placed her hands on the small body suddenly on her chest. She didn't know what this was—what to do—what to want.

"Yeah," she whispered as the baby squirmed slightly—the nurse confidently unwrapping the infant from the blanket and then gently pulling down the sheet that covered her chest. She stared at the eyes which stayed closed and tightened slightly as the rest of the body was positioned with the head right above her left breast—her lips were mere inches from the eyes and nose.

She knew the nurse said something—she heard herself give an affirmative noise. Then it was just the two of them.

81

Her and her baby—her baby.

Her baby had existed out in this world for about six hours. In those six hours she had had the baby on her—close to her—multiple times. Shortly after the birth, the baby had been brought to her chest—the little body that she had grown inside of her, that she had been waiting for. And she hadn't felt anything. Maybe she had felt something, but it hadn't been monumental—it hadn't been overwhelming joy or the purest moment of love in her life. She had felt tired and sore and weak as though her body had just pushed another body out of it.

It had felt like a whirlwind—the nurse helping her position the baby on her breast to feed right away as other activity happened around the room and to her body.

Then it had just been the three of them. He had looked back and forth between her and the baby with a glowing smile on his face—his hand either smoothing the hair on her head or caressing the baby. She was happy. She knew she was happy looking down at the cute little body that curled up to her.

But something hadn't clicked.

She didn't know her. She didn't know this baby. It was as though someone had just handed her a baby to hold and so, she held her and fed her and looked at her. But that's all there was.

Then the whirlwind continued with the handful of

visitors who had come to see them and then different nurses coming in and out for her and then the baby, then her and then the baby again. In a moment of peace, she had fallen asleep—unable to stay awake any longer.

She looked down at the face resting mere inches from hers. The baby was beautiful—perfect. As she felt the warm body against hers and acknowledged the softness of the skin, her eyes continually drifted over the beautiful face. Her hand gently moved back and forth on the baby's back—skin so soft—soft as air.

Without any other sign of waking up, the baby's eyes slowly opened—barely wide enough to truly see. The dark irises shone against the small specks of white that could be seen in the very corners of the eyes. They stared at each other. Her and her baby.

The tiny body gave a slight sigh—a puff of sweet air coming out the slightly opened lips and the eyelids closed as suddenly as they opened. She didn't know if the breath actually made it to her face—but she felt the breath of her baby travel through her as she inhaled it into her own body.

Her entire body seemed to soften from the inside out and she felt a warmth travel through her. The forehead was soft against her lips as she pressed them upon it, then moved her head back so she could once again gaze at the baby's face.

"Oh, my sweet girl." She breathed the words out rather than speaking. "I know you. I know exactly who you *are."*

08/14/2007

Hearing the upbeat cheerful greetings on the other end of the phone immediately drained her energy, causing a deep feeling of irritation that she couldn't explain. As they went through the usual—"how are you?" "how's the baby?" "how is he?"—she grabbed one of her bigger wine glasses and poured the rest of an already open chilled wine bottle into the glass. The sight of the red liquid swirling around in the glass as it filled up was somewhat meditative. She took a few sips before mentally rejoining the conversation she was currently in.

"How is nursing going?" her mother asked cheerfully. The question increased the irritation that had started to ease with her intake of wine. That's all she felt—irritation and exhaustion just ebbing and flowing at all times.

"Not great. My supply seems to be dropping and she gets frustrated a lot when I'm nursing her. We're probably going to be supplementing with formula." She could hear the lack of interest in her own voice and wondered if her parents heard it too.

"Really? Formula? That's too bad. I know babies do fine on formula, but breastmilk is just so great. And the bonding she gets from nursing—have you looked into donor milk?" She really wished her mom would stop beating around the bush and just tell her she wasn't doing this right. It would save some time. The phone call would be shorter, and she could go to bed.

"Donor milk? Like another women's breastmilk? Isn't that weird?" She could hear her dad's raised eyebrows and imagined her mom's smashed together glaring at him.

"No, it's not weird. It's milk from women who do really well at producing it to help other mothers who—don't do as well." Further irritation. She looked at the clock and did the math quickly, calculating that if she finished her glass of wine right now, it shouldn't be a problem if the baby woke up at the normal one o'clock and three o'clock times. Or should she just give up this thing that was so natural and great that she, apparently, didn't do well? The thought made her want to cry suddenly and she blinked back tears—proactively grieving no longer nursing her baby, even though she still was.

"I could look into it, Mom."

"And maybe a lactation consultant can help you and you won't even need the donor milk—"

"Do they test the milk? I mean, how do you really know if it's even breastmilk? Or what about what's in the milk? What if the woman it came from is smoking crack?" interrupted her dad, still clearly caught up on the donor's milk.

"I'd be really surprised if someone smoking crack would be producing enough breastmilk to donate it. Let alone any milk. Most women who smoke crack probably don't even make an effort to try and breastfeed or probably quit right away." She considered how much it would hurt to bang her head on the quartz countertop to the point of becoming unconscious. "Don't worry about it, she probably won't even need donor's milk. Did you look up lactation consultants to call?" Another gulp of wine went down her throat and she pressed her finger between her eyebrows.

"No. I forgot." Was that the truth? It felt like the truth. She had forgotten and, in the moments she remembered, the baby started crying or something else called her attention. Her brain was trying to process all the lists, all at the same time and everything was so scattered she couldn't do any of it. Or in those moments she remembered, she found herself unable to pick up the phone because it would mean talking to someone, scheduling an appointment, and then at some point actually getting herself and the baby out the door to go to the appointment. And her whole body was just so heavy—too heavy for any of that to be possible.

"Oh. Write it down. It could really help."

"Is that little party animal still waking you up at night?" She could hear the lighthearted tone of her dad's voice and knew his intention was not to make light of her being woken up two to three times a night for the last three months. But still—irritation.

"Yeah, I haven't really been getting much sleep."

"The joys of parenthood," he chuckled through the phone. "Parents don't really sleep again until the kid moves out". His laugh filled her head and she let out a brief noise that could have been described as a single deadened cackle.

Wonderful news. Exactly what she wanted to hear—this was her life now for the next eighteen years. What a wonderful thing to hear. She felt as if she would have been capable of slapping her dad if he was in front of her. The last bit of wine traveled down her throat.

"They say it takes a village," her mother's voice rang out. The irritation wasn't going away, and she could feel it moving up her chest. Her voice was tense in reply.

"Great." A few moments of silence. She had

nothing left to say. She wasn't going to entertain them—make them believe that this conversation had been anything but taxing. She wanted to scream at them. She wanted to scream at everyone.

"Well, we'll let you go, sweetie, so you can get to bed. Love you."

"Love you. Pass along our hugs."

"Love you too," she managed to mumble. She set the phone down harder than she meant to and it bounced a little and then slid across the counter. He walked into the kitchen with his eyebrows raised looking between her, the phone, and the wine glass.

"Why don't you go upstairs and get in bed? I'll clean up down here. Try to go get some sleep." Even with his kind words and offer, the irritation didn't ebb. She nodded and went upstairs dragging her body through the motions of going to the bathroom and brushing her teeth.

Her mom's voice kept floating through her head.

It takes a village. It takes a village.

She angrily spit out the toothpaste and slammed the toothbrush back into the holder—fuming and angrily growling to the drain at the bottom of the sink.

"Where's my fucking village?"

09/21/2007

H onking seeped through the window as it
filled the air outside. At first, it sounded like
one or two different cars responding to each other
in honks and beeps, but then quickly increased to a
pack of cars started howling in unison. She opened
the curtain slightly so she could see what was going
on directly outside the house. The light traffic had
stopped, but she couldn't see why. Her eyes darted
back and forth, up and down the road to see what
was causing such commotion.

That's when she saw the dog jumping about in
between the cars, as if getting a taste of unfenced
freedom for the first time in a while. Its brown body
could be seen every now and then as it bounced
from car to car sometimes jumping up on the doors
to peer in the windows at the startled faces looking
out.

And then the yelling started.

The voice was familiar. She had heard it often,
loudly strained over the noise of kids playing

outside. She wondered what the voice sounded like when it wasn't yelling. She had never heard it in any other form. She felt as if she should have known the kids' names by now—the kids who belonged to the voice so often heard screaming at them to get in the house or to stop doing something or to start doing something. But she never took note of the names. She just took note of the voice and registered that it was *that* woman—the woman everyone on the street knew as *that* woman. *That* house. *Those* kids. *That* shit show.

Her eyes moved back-and-forth between the cars looking for the woman producing the howls, screaming the dog's name with guttural vigor. She caught herself suddenly smiling as the thought crossed her mind: this was the original reality show. One neighbor watching another neighbor, the intimacy of one's home gone, and on view for all to see.

But then she saw her. Her stomach dropped. She felt immediate tightness in her chest. The subtle smile slipped off her face.

The woman had her hand on the dog's collar—her arm strained with the weight of the dog tugging against her. The other hand was up on her chest holding the towel which was the only thing covering her body.

She couldn't see the woman's facial expression

from this far, but she could still hear the yells that came from her mouth as she grabbed at the dog and pulled with all her might to get it to come with her. She saw the woman's head swivel around looking quickly at the surrounding cars, and then back down to the dog—never again looking up.

Finally, the dog relented. Even though her grip slipped, it started running back to the house where two of the children stood out in the front yard observing the chaos. The woman followed the dog back weaving in between the cars and then turned her voice upon the children—yelling at them to get back inside. Their little pajama-covered bodies abruptly turned and ran as fast as they could back into the house.

The cars started moving again. She could imagine what some of the drivers were thinking about the hot mess that they had just witnessed. That's what that was. Those were the words used for a woman like that: a hot mess. As they drove away, they might even shake their heads and wonder to themselves what kind of household that was—what kind of mother the woman was. What kind of woman she was. They might even go so far as to make their own assumptions and answer the questions themselves. Some of them would even laugh, wishing that they had been able to pull out their phones quick enough to take a video of it and show a friend later. For some of them, it was golden entertainment, the kind of stuff that they hear about but never got to see.

Instead of pursing her lips and shaking her head or laughing to herself and rolling her eyes, she felt the tears start dripping down her cheeks. What she saw was a woman just like her—a woman who was exhausted and overwhelmed by the life that she was living. What she saw was a woman who had maybe just been able to take a shower for the first time in a week—just a few minutes to herself to at least clean her own body. And then it was interrupted. Because it was always interrupted.

She saw the woman as someone who stood under the gaze of others and hoped with all her heart that she could just become invisible; the woman who didn't know this was how her day would start; the woman who once again thought to herself—*what will they think of me? Do they think I'm as much of a failure as I feel I am?*

Her body was overcome by sobs. She couldn't tell anymore if she was crying for the woman or for herself. She wished that she could go across the street, knock on the door, and just tell her it was okay—tell her that someone understood and that it's not her fault—tell the woman that they don't know what it's like, no one truly knows what it's like. She wished she could go and do that, but she looked down at the baby in her arms and realized that was the problem—the only people who could do that, or wanted to do that, were the ones who themselves didn't have the energy to give to anyone else.

Her fingers slowly fell from the window. The curtain dropped and she walked away.

10/18/2007

The baby's small chest moved up and down at a faster pace than her own chest could without hyperventilating, and yet the baby's breathing was still peaceful. The tiny mouth was slightly open with the balled-up fist touching the tip of the nose. She looked up from the baby girl to him, lying on the other side of the small human. He was also watching the baby breathe, a soft smile on his face—one of his fingers tracing the baby's cheek, soft and consistent enough not to disturb. She caught his eye and smiled his soft smile back at him. This was their moment—all three of them in the dimly lit bedroom on the bed just big enough and small enough for comfort. This was theirs.

His smile turned into a grin. "That was a perfect shit show of a day, wasn't it?"

She stifled a laugh filled with disbelieving pleasant exhaustion and shook her head, looking back down at the now peaceful little body between them.

"Let's go to the zoo."

"The zoo? Today?" He had looked at her as though he had heard wrong or as if she had just pulled plane tickets out from her purse.

"Yes, the zoo. Today. It's nice out and she's never been to the zoo yet. We've deprived her." Their five-month-old being referred to toppled over from a sitting position to her side letting out squeals of delight while trying to grab her own toes.

"Yes, the deprivation is clearly getting to her," he sarcastically observed. He crawled over to the baby on his hands and knees and, to the baby's further delight, started blowing on her belly. He stopped even though the baby seemed to gurgle in protestation and looked back up at her. "Are you sure you're up for it?"

She stiffened slightly at the brief twinge of annoyance that his question caused her. She was up for anything that was different than the same day-to-day monotony. The zoo was an experience that she had been excited about since she was pregnant. "Yeah, it'll be fun. It's the zoo—she'll love it!"

In the next twenty minutes, they did the synchronized, yet clunky, athletic maneuver of two parents preparing to take an infant out to a new place for a new experience.

"Do we need this?"

"Yeah, just throw it in the bag—oh no, not that,

the bag will be too full."

"How is she out of socks? Have you seen a pair of her socks anywhere?"

"What food do you think we should bring? Do you think they'll have any food there?

"Yeah, zoos usually have food. But I don't know if it's anything she'll be able to eat. Maybe some of her puff things."

"Okay, we have wipes. I put together a bottle for her, diapers—"

"How many diapers?"

"Three. Do you think that's enough?"

"Maybe do another just in case."

"Do you really think we're going to need to change her diaper more than three times in a couple hours?"

"Well, I don't know what if—I don't know."

"The diaper bag is getting pretty full."

"Do you think she'll be warm enough in that?"

"Yeah, it's like sixty degrees out. Plus, it has an elephant on it."

"Do you have everything?"

"Yeah, you got her?"

"Yup!"

The car seat buckled in. Keys jammed in the ignition. The engine whirred on. Seatbelts clicked. Mirrors adjusted. Shift to reverse, shift to drive, and they were off to the zoo.

As they walked through the big arch identifying the entrance to the zoo, paid their admission, and put on their wristbands, she could feel excitement building. They both turned often to the baby in the stroller, bending down so they were at eye level saying things like "we're at the zoo", "we're going to see so many animals", "are you excited for the animals?". The baby gurgled back at them, enjoying their uplifted voices and wide smiles.

They had a quick discussion about which exhibit to start with while looking at the illustrated map. Which one would she like best? Was it best to start at the back of the zoo and walk back? Were they going to make it through the whole zoo today? What exhibits were priorities? They decided to start big with the elephants. The baby was wearing an elephant on her shirt, so it made sense.

The stroller rattled along the paved path as kids raced by them with parents in tow. Laughter and excited squeals filled the air as animals were spotted and little arms shot out with pointer fingers eagerly identifying. Further squeals would fill the air as the animal moved around and parents' voices could be heard in response, firmly demanding that feet be removed from the bottom rung of the fence followed by the repetitive explanation that the fence was not to be climbed.

She felt a bounce in her step spurred by the

excited flutter of nostalgia in her stomach. It felt like she was eight years old again—running down the zoo paths eagerly, not wanting to miss an animal being close to the fence or the glass windows.

Intense green eyes of a tiger meeting hers in an unbreakable gaze filled her head as she remembered running up to the window before her brothers could get there. The tiger had been lying on her side in the corner with hindquarters against the wall and face against the window with one large paw pressed on the thick glass.

She had looked around quickly, her heart thumping before going under the ropes she knew she was supposed to stay behind. Her heart had been going much faster than her feet as she padded softly up to the window, the large green eyes staring intently without any movement from the massive orange body. She had knelt down and inched herself closer until her knees hit the rocky wall underneath the window—her face two inches away from the giant cat's. She had held her breath as the eyes stared out at her from white fur decorated with symmetrical black markings and surrounded by light orange which darkened down the snout to a heart-shaped pale pink nose right above soft white lips that she imagined would feel soft against her hand.

She had felt as though she had never seen a

face so beautiful, created with such a beautiful design. She could see each hair and how all of them together created the magnificent creature before her. As she stared back into the darkly lined green eyes in awe, she knew that God was an artist. Time seemed to freeze, and she felt like those eyes knew everything about her and everything about everything. She started to think her first thought was wrong—maybe God was actually in the tiger.

The tiger's left ear twitched and then the eyes blinked for the first time as she heard the patter of her brothers' feet coming up behind her. She ignored them yelling her name. Then she heard her dad yell it and she broke away—the tiger getting up at the same time. Her dad had a conversation with her about following the rules and staying on this side of the rope. He had looked at her softly after being firm.

"It isn't about us, but the animals. They may not like us getting so close. They're already in captivity—let's not make it worse." Her heart kept pulling her back to the tiger the entire time, with the dream of somehow freeing her.

She heard her name called and realized that, while lost in memory, she had walked ahead of him and the baby who whined gleefully when she turned back to join them.

"Looks like we may need to end up getting an

annual zoo pass—at least one for you, yeah?" he joked with her as she tickled the baby's outstretched fingers.

"Daddy's just having trouble keeping up, isn't he?" she cooed to the baby while giving him a smirk. The baby let out a high-pitched "eeee" in response, thumping her chubby arms on the sides of the stroller. "That's right, say come on Daddeeeee. Let's go see some elephants." She looped her arm under his and smiled up at him. "This way I don't lose you again." His lips pressed against her forehead.

"I don't mind getting lost, but let's do it together." They continued walking, both stopping at times to verify they were going the right way or questioning whether they wanted to stop at something they passed. It wasn't long though before they saw the tops of large grey bodies moving above some trees that led to the exhibit. They picked up speed and soon there they were in front of the gentle giants they had been searching for. Two elephants close by were using their trunks to pick food from a basket on a pole—their trunks controlled and reaching while they focused on their target with dark eyes framed by long eyelashes.

Both he and her moved in unison and were on either side of the baby pointing and exclaiming as she looked with an unchanging facial expression.

"Do you see the elephant?"

"Two elephants! Look how big! They're eating food."

"Look, the elephant on your sweatshirt," he gently jabbed at the baby's chest before pointing back to the elephants standing about twenty yards in front of them. "And there are the real elephants. How cool is that, baby girl?" The baby's facial expression of disinterest didn't shift.

"Do you know what an elephant says?" she asked and quickly pushed air through her closed lips while puffing out her cheeks, letting out some kind of sound she doubted anyone would have guessed was supposed to resemble an elephant. Just then a smaller elephant came running up—its ears flapping joyfully and trunk unfurling as it neared the larger ones, reaching out to one of the other's legs. "Ah! Do you see that, sweetie?"

"It's a baby elephant! Just like you. Do you see the baby elephant?" He tickled the baby slightly to get her attention and then pointed at the little elephant. Nothing. The baby's eyes started darting back and forth and she started to move her head as if requesting a different view. The little eyes began to squint, and the mouth began to open wider with the start of a well-known scream.

Without needing to consult each other, they were on the move quickly—the scream stifled by the movement of the stroller. Their excited voices were now tinged with a sense of hesitancy as they walked.

"What do you think she would like?"

"Maybe something that moves more?"

"There's a bird exhibit over there!"

"She sees birds every day though."

"What about monkeys?" They both looked at each other with renewed confidence and speed-walked over to the monkey exhibit.

A crowd of people blocked the view of the stroller as they got close to the ape enclosures within the primate house. She could see the apes swinging about to the rhythm of the murmured conversations and sudden exclamations of small voices. She was trying to scope out a spot to get closer as he knelt down in front of the baby and started making monkey sounds. The baby's short laugh could be misconstrued as a grunted cough emitted from her stroller. She saw an opening.

"Hey, come on, over there!" She jerked the stroller away and they made their move, getting up to the window in their own little corner. Apes swung from ropes, jumped from trees, and grabbed food from plates with little playful skirmishes breaking out between a couple of them sporadically.

They were on both sides of the baby's stroller

again, their necks turning quickly from the apes to the little face, back to the apes, fingers pointing.

"Look do you see the monkeys?"

"Wow, look at them swinging. So fun. See the monkeys?

"I don't think she's really looking at them."

"Look, follow my finger. See where I'm pointing? See the monkey?"

"Yeah, she is still not actually looking."

"My finger." He wiggled it close to the baby's face and then brought it closer to the window. "Follow the finger. There are monkeys in there!" He looked over at her in disbelief as the baby's eyes refused to focus on a single ape. "Do you think she can't see them?"

She rolled her eyes. "She can see fine."

"I mean, maybe they're too far away, like her eyesight hasn't developed that much yet."

"They're really not that far and it's not like they're small or staying still." Two of the monkeys chased each other across a rope right above where they were looking. "Look, sweetie! Look at them chasing each other."

The baby's eyes focused on her instead of the monkeys—the small face giving her nothing short of a scowl. At the baby's first screech she saw the people next to them jump as if one of the apes had suddenly appeared next to them. She grimaced as they hurriedly walked away with the stroller emitting sounds more reminiscent of a very angry cat.

Zebras were next, then giraffes to hippos to rhinos to lions to bears. With each new animal, and each disinterested or disgruntled response from the baby, their excitement tinged with hesitation became hope tinged with fear, slowly growing to exhausted disbelief. They were in front of the penguins who were putting on a show right in front of the baby's face as they stared through the window at an underwater world with small black bodies zooming by at high speed. As the window suddenly filled with swirling, whirling bodies it was as though a ballet of penguins was being performed just for them. She stared in awe then looked down at the baby with cautious optimism. The little mouth let out a huge yawn as the baby examined her own fingers with a sense of boredom.

"Is she broken!?" she exclaimed at him in disbelief. He peeled his own eyes away from the dance and raised his eyebrow at the stroller's occupant. "Who doesn't love the zoo?"

He bent down and looked at the baby, slowly grabbing the little fingers she was transfixed by and pointing them to the penguins. With a howl, the baby stealthily pulled away her fingers from his hand and went back to her careful examination of them. His disbelief now matched hers as he straightened up shaking his head.

"It's the only explanation. She must be broken."

The next exhibit had been in the bathroom and the subject matter was an exploded diaper. She had stood in the bathroom looking down in horror at the changing table and the red-faced screaming baby, not sure what to do. There were plenty of diapers in the diaper bag, but it was lacking in pants. They had exited the bathroom with the baby somewhat consoled and very much pant-less. He had raised his eyebrow questioning the recent development and just the word *everywhere* along with her facial expression, made him understand.

"Where are the pants?"

"In the garbage." She appreciated his lack of comment as they found their way to a bench. He was handing the baby one cheerio at a time with a dead look in his eye, and she felt a single bead of sweat drip down her back and fall uncomfortably into her pants. The baby had maintained a consistent low whine after the diaper change.

She felt that their defeat was imminent. They had been defeated. The zoo had been defeated. He leaned back on the bench next to her and shook his head letting out a sigh. They sat listening to the distant sounds of children laughing amid the faint animal sounds.

All of a sudden, a giggle erupted from the stroller and they both looked over to see a little arm reaching for something behind them as the baby's face lit up in glee. She quickly turned around to see what exhibit was behind them that she hadn't noticed. Her eyes searched wildly, but there was only a tree behind them standing tall against the zoo's fence. She turned to him confused, wanting to know if he was seeing something she didn't. His mouth gaped open as he looked from the tree back to the gleeful noise still coming from their tiny human. She looked back at the tree and saw it—poking out of the side of the tree was a small whiskered face peering at them. The little face slowly tilted, poking out a little more and the baby shrieked in excitement at the squirrel's movement. Both of them look from the squirrel to the baby in a completely new level of disbelief.

"Are you freaking kidding me?!"

The baby adjusted her head and her little mouth fell open slightly, eyes still staying closed. She felt her heart fill up just looking at the little nose and the soft eyelashes. It didn't necessarily make sense to her, but she knew she truly meant it as she looked across at him and kissed his fingertips which lay on the pillow next to her.

"It was a good day."

11/09/2007

*Y*ou *are the kind of love story I've been looking for my whole life.*

The big, beautiful eyes with softness only an infant could portray, scanned her face—the little round mouth opening with glee. She scrunched her nose at the baby and made a whirring sound with her tongue which resulted in a response of joyful gurgles.

"I'm gonna get your little neck, neck, neck, neck," she playfully growled, gently digging her face into the small space under the baby's chin and chest. She laughed when realizing how hard a task it was, as the rolls of the baby's almost non-existent chin kept the neck hidden like a warm secret treasure. She felt her lips successfully meet the object of her searching—soft with subtle sweat and untarnished by exposure to air or anything else, as it had been cradled and held away from the world by the rest of the baby's cloud-like skin. As her lips gave the skin quick little pointed kisses, a squeal let loose from the baby who squirmed with glee—the baby's little hands subtly tugging on her hair, instinctually needing to hold onto something in reaction to tickling lips and breath.

She pulled herself away from the comforting warmth with a sense of hesitancy at parting her lips from the beautiful skin, but at the same time excited to see the face capable of emitting such joyful sounds. It did not disappoint.

The baby's eyes had gone from giant circles to half-moons, shining through the sky of the little girl's face, glinting as she smiled back at them—her fingertips gently moved across the baby's ballooned belly resulting in some more squeals and gurgles. The baby's mouth opened wide—the top lip pulled back showing the pink gums hinted red on the very edge where a white shard of tooth had been making its way out. She instinctually brought her lips down to the baby's nose, forming perfectly to the rounded nub. She could stay there forever with the little nose tip hugged by her lips, the soft breath on her chin, the compact little body pressed against her chest.

The baby stilled and then began to squirm again in happy protestation about her nose being softly nibbled on. As she pulled her face away from the baby's, the chubby little hands reached out to her cheeks and held her in place only a couple inches away from those round eyes. The baby's eyes surveyed her in a way she had never felt seen before. The eyes went over every detail on her face with a sense of familiarity and wonderment, living in the same gaze at the same moment.

Little fingers gently moved from her cheeks to her eyes. As she closed her eyelids, the fingertips swept through her eyelashes, to her eyebrows, and back to her eyelids applying gentle pressure until she opened them. The baby let out a whispered coo—her voice a whispy passenger carried by her breath. The fingers found her nose and investigated the hardness of the bridge, suddenly becoming soft and then falling away into the unknown darkness of her nostrils. Tears sprang to her eyes as sharp baby nails pricked the inside of her nasal passages, and she gently removed them with a smile, placing the fingers, not even half as long as hers, upon her lips. The baby's eyes didn't show any sign of upset but continued to shine as the baby's fingertips parted her lips slightly and felt the bounce of the bottom lip. A smile erupted at the bottom lip's playfulness—the baby's mouth then opened wide bringing her face close, using the other mode of investigation of the external world. Her lips fell gently into the baby's open mouth which, even when as opened as wide as possible, was still small enough for just the middle of her lips to nestle into.

Their faces pressed together—uneven in size with her nose right at the baby's wide-open eyes and her own eyes peering into puffs of baby hair.

Her face was pushed back gently, the oral exploration phase of her complete, and the hands remained on her cheek—the eyes now widening to look down at the object recently tasted.

You are the kind of love story I've been looking for my whole life.

The thought filled her body. She wasn't even sure if it was a thought or a feeling. Or maybe it was a state of being—one that she could live in forever, if only she could pause the world.

III

Fall

11/2007

S creaming filled the room—gurgled screams that could only come from a helpless infant trying so hard to express a need and not knowing how to do so. The screams seemed to slice into her as she held the baby in her arms, going back and forth, back and forth with her whole body—feeling as if she was at the point of lunging for her life, trying to do anything to comfort the baby. Trying to do anything to stop the stabbing screams. She looked down at the face with eyes, nose, and cheeks completely squished together—the mouth open as wide as possible. The breath was fast-paced between the screams, the squished face dampened with tears, snot, and drool.

"I'm trying, sweetie," she helplessly pleaded. "Shh, shh, shh. Please. It's okay. You're okay. You just need to sleep."

She tried to stay calm. She tried to do the one thing she was supposed to do—just comfort this baby. But she could feel it welling up inside her.

115

There was a tightness that started in the middle of her abdomen and continued to spread and spread through her chest. A tightness as if her insides were being squeezed to the point of suffocation, yet at the same time bringing forth power from within her. And then she exploded.

"What do you want from me? What do you want from me?!"

The tightness held back all of the calm, squeezing to the point where only the power of true desperation could make its way through and finally break free.

"What the fuck do you want from me?! I can't do this!" she screamed—her voice drowning out all other noise.

A moment of relief as the tightness loosened.

The baby's eyes popped open at the sudden change in her voice. The face suddenly switched—eyes now orbs of fear and the mouth closed tight so that the lips were almost non-existent. She looked in those eyes and any false relief dropped immediately into the pit of her stomach. She could see the betrayal—the terror. And she knew she was everything she had not wanted to be in that moment.

It was only a moment because the eyes closed as quickly as they had opened and the baby's body shook with screams as if trying to fill her ears with the unrelenting guilt she had in her heart.

"I'm sorry, I'm sorry. I just can't." she moaned to the baby, to herself, to it all.

Her words were barely heard. She felt unsure she even said them as the screams swallowed up any other sound. Her arms acted, and she set the baby down in the crib still squirming, squished-faced and seemingly breaking.

Her feet were next to act, carrying her out the room and down the stairs. If she closed her eyes maybe she could pretend the baby wasn't upstairs crying but sleeping as the baby was supposed to—as she needed the baby to.

But the walls of the house betrayed her and, though faint, she could still hear the screams. Her hands grabbed onto her head—her fingers immediately knotted into her hair. She just needed to grab something. Her eyes stared blankly down at her feet which stood bare on the wood floor. Her heart raced as if trying to run from the tightness that was still subtly making its way through her chest. Buzzing filled her mind, quiet enough that the screaming in her mind could still be heard. It occurred to her that this might be how it feels when people lose their minds. Her body felt like it was shaking with the electricity of an adrenaline rush. Everything felt out of control.

"What am I supposed to do? How am I supposed

to do this?" Her whispers faded by the time they reached her toes. The desperation moved quickly through her lungs. "I can't fucking do this. How I am supposed to do this?!" she screamed. Her fingers pulled and the pain at her scalp urged the desperation on. She found herself at the edge of the couch, her body collapsing on it with her face breathing in the fabric. "I can't do this. I just can't do this. Help," she whispered to no one—to nothing.

She listened. She listened to her own breath now ragged from the screaming and the adrenaline. She listened to the car she couldn't see driving by the house—its driver in another world than hers. She listened to the silence. And then she heard the faint scream of the baby. And she broke.

The first scream that came from her mouth was almost like a trial scream for the chaos that had broken out inside her. It was a scream filled with frustrated exhaustion letting itself out into the world for a moment of expression. But the screams that followed ripped through her body, clawing their way out, leaving marks on her throat which were continually scratched open as the herds of turmoil continued to run out of her body.

Her hands mimicked the screams as they clawed at the couch and sometimes at her own body—becoming fists with her nails stuck into her palms and the fists, beating the rest of the flesh that belonged to her. It had taken ahold of her—she let herself be lost to it. She felt the pain in her throat and the sting on her limbs from her own beating. She heard the sound that erupted from her—purely animalistic and otherworldly in nature, bouncing around the small dark cavern made by her head and the back of the couch. She tasted her dried tongue and the saliva that would fill her mouth momentarily between screams.

She didn't know how to stop. She didn't know if she even could.

She wondered if they knew—the people in their cars. Did they hear her screaming? Did they know she was losing herself?

No one heard. No one knew.

It's as though she didn't even happen.

12/2007

"Have you had any trouble sleeping?"

Yes, sleep doesn't exist anymore.

"Well—" She instinctually gestured to the baby in the stroller next to her. "No one is sleeping real well in our house."

"Of course, I'm sure she'll sleep through the night soon. Do you experience a lack of energy?"

Yes, energy doesn't exist anymore.

"That kinda goes hand-in-hand with the no sleep thing."

"Mmhm." The nurse looked up from the chart and gave her a close-mouthed, grimacing smile before turning back to the paper on the desk. "Do you have little interest or pleasure in doing things?"

How is it possible to do more things than what's currently being done? How is it possible to want to do more?

"I mean, I don't really do many things right now. Other than taking care of her."

"Any problems with eating too much or too

little?"

"Sometimes I forget to eat in between naps and feeding her. It's just a lot to keep track of."

"You really need to make sure to eat at least three meals a day. Especially if you're trying to breastfeed."

Noted.

"Do you have feelings of hopelessness or being down?" the nurse asked, her voice the same as when asking if she still had hemorrhoids.

There's too much to feel to know what it all is.

"I feel exhausted a lot and some days are really hard. I guess—I don't know. I don't think so. I don't know."

"That's totally normal. It's just the season of motherhood you're in. Totally normal."

She placed a false smile on her face and looked down at her bitten fingernails and then over at the baby peacefully gazing at the fluorescent lights covering the ceiling.

This is normal. Just a season. What a relief.

01/2007

"I want to make you feel good," he murmured in her ear.

You can't.

It was said in her silence—tragically whispered and furiously yelled at the same time. But he didn't listen. He didn't even know there was anything to listen to.

Now it was just her and the large mirror that hung above the bathroom vanity. At one time, she had been excited to install the mirror. It was big enough to really see herself in when standing back from the sink. There was a point when she wanted to see herself.

The tip of her finger slid down her chest in between the breasts that sagged with the extra weight of milk and the use of breastfeeding. His hands had been on them, caressing them, giving subtle squeezes. She wondered if he had felt her tense when his mouth found her nipple.

In synchronization with her eyes, her robe closed

around her body as she wrapped herself. With all of her heart, she hoped the baby wouldn't wake up tonight. She couldn't let them have the same body in such different ways. How could her body even have so many uses? Be used so much by others? She looked down at the torso her arms wrapped around. Was it even hers anymore?

A small reddish-purple mark on her thigh caught her attention. She had felt his mouth sucking on her skin. So many times before, it would have thrilled her—his hands sliding over her, his mouth coming back to hers in between adventuring over her body. That night she had felt nothing.

She had resolved to let him do what he wanted. Before him, she had learned how to turn herself off during sex when needing to—becoming just a body. But she had never needed to do that with him. Never wanted to do that with him.

It wasn't even something she had to consciously do tonight. She was already disconnected. She was already just a body lying in their bed.

What is wrong with me? His tongue flicked against hers as his hand cupped her cheek.

Just let it be over soon. His head between her legs.

She felt nothing physically and felt the weight of everything emotionally—the guilt, the fear, the sadness. Was she broken?

The dread had welled up inside of her when he

had initiated the physical intimacy. His hand had pleasantly rubbed her back, down her thigh, and back up to her stomach. She told herself it was pleasant. It had been pleasant to her before. It was supposed to be pleasant. But she dreaded what was expected of her. Either it would be another night where she turned him away, mumbled an apology, pleaded for sleep, and silently fumed at someone else requesting something of her when she had so little left to give. Or she wouldn't resist—wouldn't object. The lack of objection would fuel him on because if she didn't object, tonight must be the night she wanted him.

He had pulled her close to him and brought her lips to his, savoring her taste and the physical connection. Her lips didn't kiss the way they used to. She used to love kissing him, feeling his bottom lip between her lips. The warmth, the subtle wetness. There were times in the past that she could have just stayed with their mouths pressed against each other, breathing each other in.

But her lips didn't kiss the way they used to.

She wished he wouldn't involve her in such a way. She wished he would just have sex with her instead.

The bathroom tile was cool on her feet as she walked to the toilet, cleaned herself of the aftermath, and flushed. She watched the soiled toilet paper circle the bowl and then be swept away into the darkness. When she was younger, she was always looking to be swept away in passion—swept away by the light sensation that was brought about by a hand of another cupping her cheek and lips pressing against her own.

The whooshing of the water in the toilet bowl dimmed as the rest of the water disappeared. Now she was looking to be swept away into the darkness, following the evidence of what was left of sexual intimacy.

A soft creak and movement in the mattress alerted him that she had come back into bed. He had closed his eyes feeling a sense of relief, pleasure, and release after rolling away off her. At times there were moments of doubt as he enjoyed her body and did the things he knew she liked. But the doubt would fade when he felt a slight catch in her breath or a subtle moan. He had missed her so much, had missed feeling her—being with her.

Her back was turned to him, and he could make out the outline of her curves lightly covered by the sheet. As he scooched his body closer to hers, he imagined wrapping around her and falling asleep as they typically did after sex. As his hand reached out and touched her side, he felt her flinch run up his arm like an electric shock. In the moment of her flinch, he felt the doubt flood him.

There were no words exchanged. The flinch said it

all. Her silence said it all.

He rolled onto his back and looked up at the ceiling in painful confusion and doubt—hearing an echo of words unspoken.

02/2008

The alarm didn't wake her up—it didn't even go off. It hadn't been set in nine months. It hadn't needed to be.

The baby screaming through the monitor had woken her up—her automatic reaction was a feeling of frustration and disbelief. Something in her chest clenched at the sound—the only sound she ever woke up to now. She didn't want to open her eyes—didn't want to force her body to fully wake up. She just wanted to sleep.

With the sound of a fiercer scream making the speaker of the monitor buzz a little, her eyes opened glaring into the darkness of the sheets she had pulled over her head. She just wanted to sleep.

After a few minutes of trying to drag her heavy body up from a horizontal position, she got her feet over the edge of the bed and on solid ground.

The ground didn't really feel solid. Nothing really felt solid.

The baby's face broke into a smile when she

walked into the room and the screams immediately turned to gurgled sounds of delight. Her hand caressed the baby's face which looked up at her hopefully and happily. Once lifting the baby from the crib, she held the baby against her for a few moments—the soft hair comforting against her cheek, the small body warm and pleasantly heavy yet comfortable to hold. She closed her eyes for a minute, feeling some relief from the closing of her eyelids. Just a few minutes to close her eyes—just a minute to hold the baby against her—warm, comforting—

The small body began to wiggle, and a flailing arm caught her in the face, jolting her eyes open and her body back into forced motion. They started the day.

The microwave beeped. The oatmeal was done.

The spoon went flying through the air followed by noises of glee. She got up and picked up the spoon.

Wipe around the mouth, wipe oatmeal out of the baby's hair, wipe the chair, wipe the table, wipe the floor.

The water was too hot as she rinsed the bowl. It burned her fingers.

The shapes went in the different holes. Triangle went in the triangle; square went in the square; circle went in the circle.

Block was put on top of block. One block on top of another, on top of another, on top of another.

She felt the release of her urine—heard the stream hit the water in the toilet bowl. The baby's hands grabbed at her bare thigh trying to climb her as the little voice whined and whined.

The ball bounced across the floor. Bounce, bounce, bounce.

Chubby legs kicked toward her face as she lost her grip on one of them. Hold the feet, open the drawer, grab the escaped foot. Wipe. Grab another wipe. Regain grip on the escaped foot. Wipe. Roll the diaper up. Throw the diaper away. Open drawer. Grab new diaper. "Hang on, almost done, stay still."

Read a book. Read the book again. Her head bounced as she felt herself start to fall asleep. Read the book ag—no, grab another book.

Rock, rock, rock. Sway, sway, sway.

She kissed the little nose and stared down into the baby's eyes—looking up at her with complete comfort. The baby's body curled up against her. Let the world just pause—can the world just pause?

She could sleep right here, maybe they could both just sleep right here. The wiggling started. She laid the baby down in the crib. The screaming started.

Rock, rock, rock. Sway, sway, sway.

Back down in the crib. More crying. "Sleep, baby. I love you."

The door closed. She collapsed in bed.

It all filled her—the things to do which wouldn't be done. She was too tired, and yet wouldn't sleep—couldn't sleep. She was too tired to sleep.

There were people who had called—who she should call back, but she didn't have words. She was out of the words, out of the stuff that made words. It had all left her. She felt as though suspended in a state of nonexistence—she was real, existed, but had been emptied.

Jo had called. Her voice on the message sounded happy, uplifted. Jo had asked if she wanted to bring the baby in, reminding her of their plan, that the pack n' play could be set up in the office. Come—not to work, just to see people. They wanted to see the baby—to see her. Jo had finished the message by saying "miss you".

She didn't miss Jo. She didn't have the capacity to miss people.

Even in moments of loneliness, she couldn't imagine being around others.

The baby screaming through the monitor had woken her up—her automatic reaction was a feeling of frustration and disbelief. Something in her chest clenched at the sound—the only sound she ever woke up to now. She didn't want to open her eyes—didn't want to force her body to fully wake up. She just wanted to sleep.

An angry grunt escaped her, entering the darkness, and she heard his sleeping body grumble in response—something just as clear as her own incoherent exclamation. She didn't wait to see if the baby would stop—she couldn't listen to the crying any longer.

She looked at the clock. *1:00 AM*. Again.

The small body curled up against her almost instantly, relaxed and calmed. It was dark, but she could still tell that the baby had closed her eyes—the little nose nuzzled up against her breast. She laid her head back and rocked and rocked and rocked.

Rocked and rocked and rocked.

She was aware of the baby's weight in her arms, aware of being in the chair. She could hear the baby's soft sleeping breath—in and out, in and out.

She laid the baby back in the crib and padded out of the room and down the hall. Back in bed. Covers over her. Head on pillow. Eyes closed. Sleep.

The sound of the crying made her eyes snap open, and she felt her chest clench so tightly she couldn't breathe.

"No," she sobbed. "No, you have to sleep. I have to sleep. Just let me sleep." Her hands were covering her ears—eyes clamped shut, trying to keep it all out. Keep everything out of her empty self.

"Just let her cry for a little bit, maybe she'll go

back to sleep," he mumbled sleepily next to her.

She wanted to throw something, to hit him, to tear him open as the sounds of crying tore her open from the inside out. Did he not feel it? Could he just ignore it?

Every cry tore through her body and she felt her body react physically to the sound. She couldn't avoid feeling it—the one thing she couldn't avoid feeling.

Her own sob ripped through the air as she dragged her body from the bed and took the baby in her arms.

She felt herself whimpering to the baby—pleading and whimpering, not even knowing if she was saying anything.

But she felt the weight of the baby and it was steady. It anchored her. She took a breath.

He came through the door of the room—arms out to her.

"Let me take her. You go sleep."

She tried to tell him it was fine, but all that came out was the whimpering.

"Come on, I'll take her. Go back to bed," he said with a hint of mild irritation.

She tried to explain about the steady weight of the baby in her arms—the anchor. She just needed to hold her. If she held her, it would be okay. If she held her and could comfort her, it gave her the last bit of purpose she had.

"Come on." He reached out and started taking the baby from her arms—removing the weight, removing her anchor.

"No," she whimpered. "Please don't take her. No, please don't take her." Tears rolled down her cheeks as her hands couldn't keep a grip on the baby, as her arms were too weak to do anything but release the last thing she had a hold of.

"Stop, you need to sleep. I've got her."

"No," she whimpered pleadingly. And then the weight was gone. He had taken the baby from her. Her arms were empty and there was nothing left—nothing left for her to do, for her to be, for her to hold on to.

Her body walked out of the room. Her body walked down the hall. Her body walked to the bed.

It collapsed—and her with it. Everything shook within her, and tears flooded her eyes, drenching her cheeks—the slight salty taste of snot and tears on her tongue.

She didn't know what was happening to her—what had happened to her. The emptiness pulled at her insides as if a hand was reaching out of a blackhole and grabbing everything it could within her—pulling it all into oblivion.

An urgent feeling gripped her—she had to go. She had to get out—had to leave before she was swallowed whole. She wasn't even sure what going meant. She just had to go.

Slowly, sleep dimmed her awareness of the tears, of the shakiness, of the blackhole swallowing her from the inside. One last sob of exhaustion came from her body before sleep wrapped its arms around her and cradled her into submission.

03/2008

Silence filled the house, wrapping itself around her like the arms of an old friend giving comfort that she forgot had been missing. Silence. No crying. No other voice. No other human-emitted noise. Silence.

Her body slowly lowered to the couch—melting into the cushions when reaching it. She laid her head back and stared up at the white ceiling decorated with a shard of yellow sunlight that snuck through the tall windows. A sigh released from her chest and out through her mouth. She was alone. A deep breath and then release. She was alone. Another deep breath and then release. She was alone.

This time it hit her. The silence no longer held her but gripped her instead. She was alone. He had taken the baby with him. When she listened closely, his encouraging words still hung in the air almost ominously.

"Just take some time for yourself. Take the

135

day. I've got her, we'll be fine." His lips smiled softly under furrowed brows and concerned eyes as he backed out the door with the car seat and diaper bag in hand. She knew his words were kind and intentions good, but as he shut the door the emptiness inside of her felt emptier.

What was she supposed to do? They had told her—the friends, the family, the doctor—do something for you. Take care of yourself. Fill your cup. Self-care. The words whirred in her head to the point of being meaningless. They had also mentioned ideas. Take a walk. Take a nap. Go grab some coffee. Go shopping. Read a book. Take a bath. Get a manicure. Whirring in her head. Do something for yourself. Fill your cup. Take a nap. Self-care. Read a book. Take a bath. Take care of yourself. Grab coffee. Do something for yourself. Go shopping. Get a manicure. Self-care. Self-care. Self-care. Whirring and whirring and whirring.

How? The thought caught her. She felt herself experience a physical reaction. Her tongue seemed to dry almost immediately and became stuck in her throat. The muscles of her body tensed and the empty feeling in the middle of her abdomen gaped as though a loosely sewn wound reopened. Her eyes searched the room around her for an answer.

How? How was she supposed to do any of those things?

They seemed alien to her, tasks that used to be so normal for her mind and body to initiate and complete. Now they seemed daunting—impossible. How was she supposed to do any of it?

A sharp pain in her bladder resulted in her ending up in the bathroom—feeling the warm water run through her hands as the roar of the toilet echoed against the tiled walls. The orange bottle on the side of the sink caught her eye and she grabbed it instinctually—pushing and twisting the cap, pouring one pill out into the palm of her hand. The first time she held one of the pills in her hand a week and a half ago she had felt internally lifted by hope as though something in her had slightly lightened. Now she just felt a weight in her chest while looking down at it—the weight of unfulfilled hope tinged with frustration and a pang of unexplainable guilt.

"How have you been feeling?" the doctor had asked glancing her over. She felt uncomfortable and suddenly doubted how sure she was of having this conversation. Her voice just seemed so quiet to her own ears as if the ability to talk any louder was gone.

"I'm just not myself. I'm just having a hard time. My husband asked me to talk to you after a bad day I had this week—a couple days ago."

"Can you explain more about what you've been feeling?" She lifted her eyes slightly to the doctor who was back to reading through her chart. "What do you mean by a bad day?"

Her insides twisted.

The ringing of his phone cut his attention from the sentence he was reading. His eyes still remained on the words—trying to get to the end of the sentence before completely detaching to answer the phone. He mumbled the words out loud to himself as though it would make him read more quickly while giving the phone a sideways glance, begging for its patience.

"The contract attached appears to be missing—clause. What clause?" The ringing continued as he mumbled to himself before reaching over and grabbing the phone from its dock. "Okay, okay." He was surprised to see her name on the caller ID.

"Hey, what's going on?" At first, the silence that answered confused him, and he was about to say something again when he heard that there wasn't just silence coming through the receiver but raspy, almost airless, breathing. Concern gripped him. "Hon, are you there? What's going on?"

A sob ripped through the phone along with more erratic breathing which made the words stumbling through the receiver hard to hear.

"I can't—I need—can you—" Another sob filled his

ear and he felt himself grip the phone harder as if it would help him decipher the noises coming through.

"Okay, I need you to take a breath. I can't understand you. Can you take a breath? Is everything okay?" His voice had an edge to it, though not with frustration, but rather with adrenaline rushed instinct. Was the baby okay? Did something happen? What was happening?

The breathing became sharp as though her lungs were trying to catch the air and slow its consumption to a normal pace. The few seconds it took for her to speak again seemed an eternity.

"I can't—I did it—I—I—I shook her." The last few words seemed to explode from her followed with unrelenting sobs.

"You shook her?" he repeated her words not understanding what she could be talking about. "What do you—"

Then it hit him. She shook her. The baby. She shook her.

Panic lept through his body. "Is she okay?" His voice hardened and became louder out of instinct. "I need you to talk. Is the baby okay?" He felt his eyes dart back and forth at his desk in front of him. He had stood up out of his chair without realizing it. Was the baby hurt? Did they need to go to the doctor? He had to run over to his boss's office. He had to leave. A slight tinge of fear. Would his boss be okay with it? A bigger tinge of fear. What if the baby wasn't okay?

139

"I think so—I just—need—you—come—home." The words barely seemed to make it out of her, but it was enough.

"I'm coming." He hung up the phone and then clicked the save button and exited the window on his computer. He had gotten a small amount of relief from her words, but his adrenaline still rushed. *What had happened? What was happening? What was going on with her?* His head filled with thought after thought as he ran out of his office and down the hall to his boss's door wondering what he was going to be walking into at home.

She gulped in response to the doctor's question. She could tell her—tell her about always feeling on edge, how she loved that baby so much, but it didn't matter. It didn't seem to qualm her bouts of rage or moments where she just wanted to sink into the couch and never be found again. She could tell her about how she was finding herself snapping, yelling at the helpless child, and then what happened just a couple days ago.

She wasn't even sure how it happened. She had just needed the screaming to stop.

Please just stop.

Damnit, just shut up!

The grip of her fingers had hardened and before she knew what she was doing—she shook.

Everything inside of her had broken—fallen along with her body to the floor—holding the baby against her chest in horror. She had said sorry a dozen times within a few seconds, but it didn't matter. It still happened and with that realization, she stopped being able to breathe.

The baby was whimpering, but through her own tears, she could see that nothing else seemed apparently wrong—except everything, everything seemed wrong.

She pressed her lips, saturated with tears and snot, to the baby girl's forehead hoping that she would know—the baby would know that she did nothing wrong. But she couldn't breathe—her breath kept escaping her through the sobs. She laid the baby in the crib, hearing herself repeat, "Mommy's sorry, mommy's so sorry. I'm so sorry" over and over again between sobs as if all other words had left her—fallen out her and shattered with her heart.

The doctor was looking at her again, patiently waiting for an answer. She couldn't tell her. How could she tell someone that? The resolve she had coming into the office to tell the doctor everything faded away into the dark prison inside of her, barred with shame and guilt.

"I'm not really sure how to explain it," she whispered. Her doctor had nodded at her then looked back at the chart.

"Let's start you on an antidepressant and see how that helps you."

They would see how it would help her. She had heard it as a promise—the promise of some help and she had become hopeful. She looked at the pill with a sense of disgust. It hadn't helped, nothing had changed. Thoughts filled her head as she continued to stare at it—thoughts that filled her head but weren't concrete enough for her to grab on to. Except one that hit her suddenly: maybe it wasn't the pill—maybe it was her.

All of it drained from her. All of it. Everything in her. The thing that was supposed to help couldn't even help her. She was beyond help. She was unfixable. This was how it would be. This was who she was now—the kind of mother she was, the kind of mother she'd never thought she'd be. The medication wasn't fixing it. It was all her fault.

Her body moved mindlessly as she went into the bedroom and pulled out the bag at the back of their closet. Her hands grabbed at clothes without thought from her dresser drawer and stuffed them in the bag. There weren't any thoughts—just her body moving mechanically until her eyes swept over a picture on her nightstand. She froze.

A woman she didn't recognize beamed down at the small face of a newborn. The back of the woman's head was being cradled in the palm of his hand as he leaned over her shoulder—a soft smile full of love lay on his lips as he looked down at the baby.

She knew the woman was her. It was a fact—but she didn't feel it. And the baby. She felt a ball in her throat that she couldn't swallow. Tears flooded her eyes. The baby—so perfect and precious—her very heart outside of her body. That baby deserved the woman in the picture—the woman who could love her unconditionally, who was able to give her all the kind of love and safety she deserved.

Her cheeks were now wet with tears as she stood in the middle of their bedroom not knowing how to move with the weight of it all dragging on her limbs—not know what she was doing, where she was going, when she'd be back. She didn't know how to be that woman anymore. She didn't even know if she was capable. Somehow, someway, without even knowing how, she had lost her—had lost herself. Her voice was choked as a whisper was carried on her breath.

"I'm sorry."

As she turned away with the bag in her hand, she realized she didn't know who exactly she was saying sorry to—to him, the baby, the woman? It made sense to her to say sorry to them all.

2008

All the love stories were a lie. It rang through her and around her from inside her chest to the dark ceiling above. It wasn't that love stories didn't exist, but the telling of them was a lie. Or maybe the characteristics attached to love stories were false—mismatched for something else—something more human than love.

The first time she had laid down on the motel bed she remembered how firm and uncomfortable it was. It felt as if she was lying on a board instead of a mattress. She had buried herself under the sheets and stiff comforter, melting away into the stuffy darkness. She wasn't sure how much time had passed. Subtle shifts in the light had occurred through the cheap blackout curtains separating the motel room from any life occurring outside the window. Her clothes clung to her body as the temperature had risen at some point and made all her layers stifling. She hadn't moved though. The covers still weighed her down, her clothes somewhat twisted, tight on her skin. The dark ceiling hadn't moved either.

Love stories filled her head—the characteristically false love stories. Wasn't the ideal love story supposed to entail desire above all else? A desire for someone to be yours, the desire for someone to want you as theirs, the desire to be something that someone needs. And nothing else would matter.

The desire would mix with passion and having someone be yours would come before all else—all other connections, all other values, all other ambitions. If it was a love story, this love would be everything. There may even be heartbreak, because a true love story has too much passion, too much intensity. To really feel love there must be pain.

People would move on from each other, but still hold the other hostage by pining away or having brief moments of pause where regret and wonder would fill them—wondering if the other person stopped in the same moment and thought of them. If it was a true love story they would live in this captured love for the rest of their lives or find each other again—the time passed wouldn't matter—the lives built and lived in the interim wouldn't matter. Because if it was a love story, this love would be everything.

Her brow furrowed as she tried to look deeper into the dark ceiling as if it wasn't just a flat surface, but something that would break away and give her some kind of answer, some kind of explanation. Maybe the right word was written up in the darkness—the word that was really supposed to be used to describe those stories. It wasn't love. She knew now it wasn't love. Love didn't look like that, even though it was the most common way love was described.

But then she thought of the baby's soft fingers gently folding around her own in a sleepy instinctual reaction. Love fit that story. If love fit any story—it was that one. But when told, that love story was incomplete.

The love story between a mother and her child was told as this magical unwavering connection—a bond as no other. A love story filled with nothing but gratitude because if you weren't continually grateful, it must not mean love. It must not mean real motherhood. It must mean some kind of defect. It was a love story personal and intimate, but belonging to everyone else to comment upon and judge. It was a love story that comes with fear—fear of not loving enough, not loving the right way.

The way love was talked about in the context of this story, she found to be true. It was indescribable and powerful beyond belief. But it wasn't the full story. The story left out the guilt, the exhaustion, the fear, the confusion, the desperation, and, buried deep in the dark never to be talked about, the rage and regret.

She brought the stiff comforter up over her head again and turned over onto her side hugging her knees. Her chest shook with shallow breaths as the tears began to roll down her cheeks—collecting and spreading out among the rough fibers of the pillowcase. She was part of the most beautiful love story.

How would the story end if love wasn't enough?

IV

Winter

Date Unknown

The proximity to the motel was one of the main highlights of the bar. Not only was it possible for her to stumble the short distance back to the motel she had trapped herself in for the last two weeks—but the bar matched its neighbor's dinginess—and the dinginess matched the internal state of its occupants. Even if a handful of them still appeared put-together on the outside—just as how the motel sign was recently replaced giving the illusion that the inside of the rooms would follow suit—there was still that staleness inside. Still a void that was small enough to stay unnoticeable initially but, when seen, seemed to swallow up the rest of the entire space. Her fingernail scratched the already scratched bar top. The main highlight of the bar was that it existed for one reason, and everyone was there for that reason: to fill the void even if only for some temporary moments.

She looked down at the small shot in between her fingers. The surface of the amber liquid held a slight blur—a slight discoloration which was in fact her reflection. She felt like a blur.

She had been feeling like a blur for too long. Like a wisp of a human, moving through the air around people who were truly living. Every now and then the particles of her wispiness would catch on the arm of another or an object of what felt like a past life. She tried to hold on—tried to stay with the living—but she would drift away, blown by an unfelt breeze, leaving more of herself than she could take with.

She had been trying to make it back, but the longer it took the more impossible it seemed.

She lifted the glass to her lips and sipped slowly. She didn't want to throw the shot back in one solid motion. She wanted to feel the continuation of the burn. It was the burn she would hold onto.

He was easy to spot from across the bar. She didn't know if she actually spotted him so much as sensed him—as though desperate sadness produced a chemical that could be felt in the air. It reminded her of a male dog being able to detect a female dog in heat from over a mile away—the kind of obsession that the female dog becomes in the male dog's mind to the point that he may stop eating and become frantically aggressive trying to get to her. She felt it was the same for desperate people—when they sensed each other they became their only focus; how to get close to them; how to feel their desperation mix; how to connect to somebody the only way they had left to connect.

He was one of those who still presented well. One who still showered on occasion and looked in the mirror either hurriedly before leaving a residence or before flipping the car visor back up and pushing open the car door. But she could see it in his shoulders and, even from a slight distance, she could see it in his eyes. Even more so when they met hers.

* * *

The door handle of the single-person bathroom dug into her side for a moment as she shifted her body over. The pressure of his body pressed her further up against the metal door as their mouths aggressively sought each other—one of his hands on her waist—the other cupping the back of her neck—her hands tugging on his belt. All she could feel was the physical reaction of her body—her muscles tingling and tensing—slight pain from his teeth on her lip—the cool button of his jeans beneath her thumb. All other feeling had left her, and she let them go.

She couldn't have even told anybody what shirt

she had been wearing as it was thrown on the bathroom floor. Her pants were shed just as easily—tossed aside as if they hadn't really been important in the first place. Tossed aside with everything in her life. There it lay on the cement floor stained with dirt and grime, uncared for and dismissed as unimportant.

They sucked on each other's lips a little longer, his hands running all over her body, his fingers tweaking little parts of her and her hand already moist from stroking him. She turned herself around and bent herself over the toilet, her hands pressed on the cool ceramic tank while holding the weight of her upper body. As he adjusted himself, preparing to thrust into her, she realized the toilet lid had been removed.

The black hole at the bottom of the bowl stared up at her—reminding her of the only place left she had to go.

04/03/2008

The touch on his shoulder made him jump, but his mother's hand stayed steady. He hadn't even realized enough time had passed for his mother to get the baby ready for bed and down in her crib. It felt like just a second ago he had held his daughter's forehead against his lips, trying to let her know with every fiber of his being that it would be okay. Trying to believe it, with her small body in his arms and the softest skin against his lips. He had stayed on the couch and was not aware of a single thought or feeling until his mother's touch seemed to awaken him from his conscious nightmare.

There had been many offers of alcohol today. Before the funeral, during the funeral, after the funeral. People seemed to be keen on him not having to feel the dark mass of feelings storming within. He had declined all the offers. He wanted to be present for the baby, even though she had no idea what was going on. Maybe it wasn't that he wanted to be present for her, but rather needed to be present to her—the only thing that made any sense right now.

"I'm going to go. All the leftover food is in the fridge and the kitchen is cleaned up. Little Angel was tired from the day, so she went down easy. Hopefully, she'll sleep through the night." He nodded his head. His mother had been staying over for the past week and a half since he had gotten the phone call. He felt genuine appreciation for her but was ready to have a moment without someone trying to make everything seem okay. "I left the monitor in your bedroom. You should go to sleep. Sleep in your bed, not on the couch. You'll sleep better."

"Okay," he sighed hoping to appease her. He was finding it difficult to sleep in their bed with all of her stuff still sitting on her nightstand, waiting for its owner to come back or giving him the false thought that maybe she never left. "Thank you, Ma. You can go."

"I can make you a little more food before I go."

"No, I'm not hungry. I ate what you gave me earlier. Thank you." He was ready for this day to end.

"Okay. Promise me you're not going to sleep on the couch." He was starting to bristle. Who was she to ask him to promise her something after a day like today?

"I won't sleep on the couch, Ma."

"I'll come over early tomorrow and get breakfast together for you."

"I'm capable of making my daughter breakfast. I'm not helpless." He snapped in a moment of rage. His mother's hand shot away from his shoulder as if bitten by a wild animal.

Rage hung in the air heaving—stifling any other words. Breath was held—stuck in both his and his mother's chests waiting to see if the toxic cloud would dissipate. Intense guilt overcame him. He couldn't turn to look her in the eye. "I'm sorry, Ma. I didn't mean to snap at you. I'm sorry."

"I didn't mean you couldn't make breakfast. I just thought it might be nice to not have to worry about anything like that." Her defensive words were dripping with hurt. He knew she was trying to be helpful, trying to be there for him in a situation that didn't make sense—fix a problem that would never be fixed.

"I know, Ma. I'm sorry I didn't—I'm just tired and it's been a long day. Go ahead and come over to make breakfast. That would be helpful." Her hand wasn't as soft on him as before while she patted his back. He knew she would still be bristling slightly from his reaction and he continued to stare at his hands to avoid her face.

"Okay, I'll be here early then. I'll just let myself in

so you don't have to worry about getting up for my sake. Are you sure you don't want me to just sleep here?"

"No, you should go home. You've helped enough nights. She'll sleep fine." He wanted her to go. He needed to stop feeling her flutter around him with worry and determination to make everything seem fine.

"I'm not concerned about Avery." Her voice softened as her hand applied more pressure to his back.

"I'll be fine, Ma." He tilted his head to the side slightly so he could more directly address her while subtly keeping himself from really looking at her. "Really, thank you. You can go. I'll be fine." She cleared her throat and made a sigh of unwilling surrender. Her lips pressed firmly against the top of his head and then her hand was gone. Words of "see you tomorrow" floated through the air as he heard her gather her things in the kitchen, hesitate in the hallway and close the front door behind her.

It was only then he knew it was safe to look up. It was safe to look up and not catch anyone's eyes. Not see anyone and to not see anyone seeing him. The day had been full of glancing up and seeing someone looking at him, who would then typically glance away or provide him with a soft pitying smile. He supposed it was typical for the spouse at a funeral—the day was just a series of glances. Most of the words spoken to him were saturated in pity with a tinge of confusion. Everyone was confused about what had happened. He was confused about what happened.

He pulled himself off the couch with a great amount of effort and lumbered into the kitchen feeling drunk off of exhaustion and grief. The kitchen looked fuzzy around the edges—not blurred—but with a texture uncharacteristic of the hard edges of counters and cabinets. It also seemed like it wasn't real. Maybe none of this was real.

Please, God, don't let it be real.

His hand moved roughly over his eyes, trying to clear his vision. His hand smelled like sweat and he wondered when the last time he washed his hands was. All day his hands had shook other's or been held for a few minutes as if the other hand was gaining comfort from trying to comfort his—even though his hand had laid there limply, as numb as the rest of him. Everything looked a little sharper when he opened his eyes, and he made his way over to the sink letting the cool water run over his hands before reaching for the soap. It took him a second to realize after pushing down the plunger that his hand was still soapless. Another push and another push and nothing came out other than a squelchy noise that a full soap dispenser didn't make. He felt the rage once more quickly travel to the surface and boil over as he threw the dispenser across the kitchen.

"Is everything gone? Is that what's happening!? Everything's just fucking broken and gone!" The energy of his yell scraped the inside of his throat. His entire body shook as he had to gasp for air. Silence answered him. Just as quickly as the rage had empowered him, it left, and his back slid down the cabinet. Arms crossed on top of his knees, he brought his forehead down on his forearms feeling himself subtly tremble. There was just darkness staring at him from the cave between his abdomen and folded legs.

He didn't know what to do. There was too much whirling around inside of him and at the same time everything was muted, nothing was loud enough because the nothingness stifled it all—except for the rage. The rage seemed to be forever stirring, waiting for a chance to get enough of a breath and then claw its way through everything else, race up his bloodstream and wrap itself around his mind, constricting until all that was left for him to do was explode.

Why would she do this to them? To him. To herself. To their daughter. His breath caught in his lungs whenever he thought of the baby. His baby. Her baby. Their baby. How could she have left her? How could she have left her? Pain shot through his elbows as he realized his grip on them was tightening and tightening.

When she left, he had been worried—worried about what was going on, about what it meant. She had just left. He had come home, and she was gone. He remembered her voice on the phone when she had finally called him back. It was a voice he didn't even recognize—void of any emotion.

"I can't do it. I'm just making things worse and ruining your lives." The words had shocked him. They weren't the kind of words or thoughts that belonged to her, and he went into a speech refuting the heavy claims she had made in just a couple short sentences. Her response had been a quiet, "you don't understand", which was the first time he started feeling the anger. He wanted to beg her to help him understand. He offered time off work; asking his parents to watch the baby for a couple days, they could go somewhere together; he'd take her to see her doctor again, maybe they could increase her dosage, maybe they could try a different medication. His offers were shut down with her ominous "I can't".

What did that mean? What couldn't she do? Why? What did it mean? The phone call had ended with him telling her to take some time for herself. After pressing her, she had said she would call friends, Jo, maybe reach out to her brothers, her parents.

"Just take some time and do what you need to get better. I love you," he softly pleaded.

"I'll take some time and get better. I love you too." The reply had brought him some relief, some hope. It wasn't until a couple weeks later when he felt he was losing his mind replaying every conversation they had ever had, that he recognized the flatness in her voice. His heart had sunk as he realized that the last words he had heard from her, which had given him hope, were in fact just her repeating his words back to him, telling him what he wanted to hear.

He had kept calling and kept calling and she had kept not answering and kept not answering. It had been such a confusing time—he hadn't known what to think, wasn't sure what to tell people or who to tell anything. He wanted to give her privacy if that's what she needed but the people in their lives were starting to not be satisfied with his explanation of "she went to go take some time for herself", "I'm not sure where exactly", "I haven't heard from her lately", "No, I don't know when she's coming back". Their silence to his answers were telling, and when he finally told their parents the extent of how lost in the unknowns he was, the silence was taken over by more questions, suggestions, arguments, more suggestions, and then an accusatory silence that filled the air.

At the police station, he had felt ashamed by the lack of information he could give them.

"Any idea where she is?"

"No."

"Any idea what physical or mental condition she is in?"

"Not currently. She started antidepressants given by her doctor a couple weeks before she left."

"When was the last time you talked to her?"

"Sixteen days. I have been calling every day for the last fourteen with no response."

"What did you talk about?"

"She said she felt like she was ruining our lives. She said she can't. She said she needed time to get better."

"Was there anything that happened in the household recently that would make her want to leave?"

"No."

"Are you aware of anyone she might be staying with or signs of her having a relationship outside of the marriage?"

"No."

"Has she done anything like this before?"

"No."

"Does she have a history of suicide ideation or attempts?"

"No."

"Have you looked for her at any places she may be?"

"Yes." He listed the handful of places.

"Are there any other places you think she may be that are familiar to her?"

"No."

The blood had drained from his face as he was told she would be classified as a current missing person and their goal in finding her was to do a wellness check. His body had started shaking as the officer explained that if she was found not presenting any safety concerns, he would be notified that she was safe; however, her location would not be disclosed if she voluntarily left.

She voluntarily left. She voluntarily left.

The officer's voice had echoed in his head for five days until the phone rang and he was asked if he was her husband.

The air in the dark hole formed by his own body had become stifling as he continued to breathe in and out sucking his own stale expelled air. They hadn't really given him a definitive answer because they said they didn't have one. Her body had been filled with much more of her depression medication than it should have been, along with alcohol. Could it have been suicide? Yes. Could it have been an accidental overdose? Yes.

He had tried to be there - in the motel room where she was found unconscious not breathing by a housekeeper. They had gotten her heart to beat again, but it had been still for too long. He had tried to imagine how she accidentally overdosed. Was she drunk and kept thinking she hadn't taken her medication? Every hour or so she would have the thought *I didn't take my medication*, and then go and pop another unneeded pill. Or did she think a higher dose would help, so she just took more?

Or—

Without warning, the memory of holding his baby to his chest hit him, not wanting to let go—not knowing if anything he was doing was right, and with reluctance, slowly bringing the wide-eyed ten-month-old down to her mother's chest. The tubes had been removed, but her body was still warm, not yet stiffened by death. With one arm still supporting the small body, he let the baby's cheek rest on her skin where the nurses had pulled down the sheet slightly. The baby had made a soft sound of familiarity and her short fingers had reached up to the lips that wouldn't be able to kiss them—

A sob ripped him open, and his body tipped over onto the kitchen floor—his fingers sprawled trying to grip onto the flat tile. He laid on the ground and let it rip through him—the pain, the anger. Why did she do it? Why did she leave them? Why did this happen?

Oh, God. Oh, God, why did this happen?

He didn't know how long he laid there. Long enough to where there was nothing left. His body was too exhausted. He was limp and became aware of the cool kitchen floor against his cheek, along with his dampened skin from snot and saliva.

But he couldn't stay on the ground—he knew that. His daughter needed him to show up. His anger existed as a light simmer as he pushed himself up onto his feet. She couldn't show up—so he needed to. That was the difference between him and her.

His head pulsed as he started walking. It had been too long of a day, and he needed to sleep. He felt as though he hadn't slept since she left.

As he was about to flick the light switch, he saw the soap dispenser on the floor and flinched as he realized how glad he was that it was made from plastic and not glass. He brought the bottle back over to the sink and, as he set it down, realized that he had never known their soap dispenser to be empty before. He realized that he wasn't even really sure where the extra soap was kept or if there was any in the house. He realized he had never had to think about it. He realized that the soap hadn't been magically refilling itself over the years. Any remaining smoldering embers inside of him sizzled out with the soft shower of guilt that fell from his heart.

He fearfully recognized there may be so much more for him to realize.

10/04/2014

T he special plates were out on the table—the plates that were only used when family from outside the home came over. As his fork stabbed the food on his plate, he wondered when his mom had started using the special plates for when they came over. When had the transition occurred where he was seen as family from the outside coming in, rather than family that was just part of the home? He felt like he would have noticed the transition from eating off the same worn plastic plates—marked with the many different knife and fork marks from when an eater became too vigorous with their utensils—to the special plates made from stoneware with subtle designs and much less prone to displaying their wear and tear.

"It is so nice for you to be back in the office full-time. Do you have enough clothes to wear?" His attention eased away from the plates and wrapped around his mother's question quizzically.

"Enough clothes, Ma?"

"Yes, enough clothes to wear into the office. It's been so long since you've been going into the office full time." He managed to not roll his eyes. He wondered if mothers ever saw their sons as competent adults who could take stock of their own clothing and dress appropriately without assistance. "I'll buy you some nice shirts and a few more pants."

"You don't need to. I have clothes, Ma. It's not like I haven't gone into the office at all in the last six years. I'm wearing the same clothes I was wearing when Avery started going to kindergarten. I was going into the office then. Maybe not for a full day, but I still had to wear clothes." He smiled with his last words trying to deflect any possible annoyance that came out.

"I see Daddy wear clothes every day." The confidently spoken testimony of the seven-year-old next to him made both him and his parents smile. She proudly surveyed their reactions to her contribution to the conversation.

"That's a relief. The problem is settled then." His dad's eyes twinkled as he directed his verdict to the little girl.

"I know Daddy has clothes, but I'm wondering if he has enough work clothes", stated his mother to her granddaughter in a kind yet pragmatic tone before shooting her eyes back to him. "If they are really six years old, do they still fit? They must be worn out or out of style by now." He almost didn't manage to keep his eyes from rolling this time but was distracted from his exasperation by his daughter turning her body fully toward him and looking him up and down with her little brow furrowed, creating the only lines on her smooth face. She then lifted the tablecloth so she could get a good look at his pants and shoes before straightening herself back in her seat, seeming satisfied with her assessment.

"Well?" Her eyes met his in response as she smiled, but also noticeably straightened herself up to give her report.

"I don't think your clothes look old, but I think you might look better in other clothes." He felt his eyebrows shoot up and a chuckle escape him as he stabbed a piece of chicken from his plate and brought it to his mouth. She put her hand on his leg under the tablecloth which made him look over at her, now very serious, face. "You look nice, Daddy. Maybe Grandma should buy you clothes though." Out of the corner of his eye, he could see his mother's smile which was contained, yet still quite noticeable. He shook his head and squeezed the little hand on his leg with his own.

"I'm going to insist you go someday after school when you're with Grandma. She might need your assistance so I stay looking nice." The little head gave a single nod of an affirmative before going back to leaning over her plate as she stuffed a forkful of broccoli in her mouth. The top of the floret stuck out of her lips like a blossoming tree as he ran his palm over the top of her head.

"We'll have to find a good day." His mom lowered her body and slightly leaned in closer to the little girl with a mischievous and much too satisfied smile. Her eyes darted to him gleaming with additional satisfaction before she straightened herself back up. "Now that you have so many activities going on, I don't get to see you as much after school, but we'll find a day to go shopping just the two of us. Have you made new friends in the playgroup you're in?

"It's a theater group, Grandma, not a playgroup. We perform plays, but we're called a theater group. Right, Daddy?"

"Right," he assured her.

"We could be called a playgroup because we put on plays." The little girl's face now went into thoughtful consideration as her hand still clasping her fork slowly stabbed at the broccoli left on her plate. "But there are different groups that play things, but don't put on plays. If people just heard playgroup, they might think it's just a group that plays. Not a theater group. We don't want other kids to be confused, so we're called a theater group, Grandma." He watched as she mulled the thoughts around in her head, voiced them, and then looked confident in her conclusion. He could see how his mom was somewhat put off by being thoroughly corrected, but maintained her polite smile through it all.

"Ah, okay, a theater group. That's what I meant. Have you made new friends in your theater group?" his mom asked somewhat tersely with emphasis on the word *theater*.

"I do have a new friend." The little girl happily wiggled in her chair, excited about being able to share something that made her happy, and not at all put off by how her explanation wasn't warmly received. "Her name is Molly, and she has a backpack with a picture of her dog on it. She lives just with her dad." The excitement in her body lessened and she looked back to her plate where broccoli hung on the tines of the fork. "Her mom got cancer. She died. Just like mine."

"Not just like yours." He felt his body tense as his mother's slightly lowered comment floated across the table. He didn't even breathe.

Please don't let her have heard it. Please don't let her have heard it.

"What do you mean, Grandma? My mom died too." The little girl's head bent slightly, and a look of concentration settled on her face—ready to try and understand an explanation sure to be given. He looked at his mother out the side of his eye as she looked up with a craftily placed expression of surprise on her face, as though shocked she spoke loud enough to be heard.

"Ma—" He kept his voice soft, but firm trying to let the warning not come out threatening yet still effective.

"Yes, dear, but your friend's mom passing away from cancer is different. She got cancer. She didn't choose—"

"MA!" His hand stung as it hit the table causing the dishes to subtly clink against the wood, suddenly awakened from their existence of merely holding food and drink. He felt himself fuming. Why did she have to be this way? What was wrong with her? He knew his face now portrayed the threat he should have originally made, but his mother's sharp eyes pierced him holding their own. Now he had crossed a line.

"Am I saying something incorrectly? Is there something I'm missing? She chose to leave. She could have been strong and gotten through just like the rest of us do." He glanced down at the little girl next to him wondering if he could somehow have the words she just heard surgically removed from her brain.

Maybe she wouldn't understand. Maybe that was worse – so often the misunderstanding was worse.

He was suddenly exhausted instead of enraged as he watched his mother grow in her anger at being yelled at in her home.

"Please, Ma. Stop—" he pleaded.

"Guess what? Being a parent is hard. Too bad. You do it. You stick around and be there for your family because nothing is more important. And if there is something more important or you're too selfish, well then maybe what happened was—"

His father's voice raced through the air, pushing his own aside, yelling his mother's name and then quickly discarding English as the two spat at each other in their first language from across the table for a handful of seconds before falling into steely silence. He dared to take a silent breath as his parents glared at each other and then went back to eating. It all ending as quickly as it began.

The table was cloaked in tense silence. He felt himself slightly shake as he breathed deeper than normal—his mother's words echoing in his head.

"The dog on her backpack is actually her own dog," the little girl exclaimed suddenly. "They took a picture of her dog and put it on her backpack. I think it was printed. But it's her own dog". The little girl looked around at all of them wanting to make sure they fully understood the concept. He grabbed her hand on the table next to his and squeezed it gently. Her eyes met his with a hint of relief that calm responses still existed in the world.

"Sounds like a pretty cool backpack."

* * *

After a few minutes of driving, he realized that his fingers were sore from clenching the steering wheel. He didn't understand why his mother decided anything she said had been necessary, when she knew for a fact the evening could have existed much better without it. What was he supposed to do with her? He would have to have a conversation with her. That would go well. He was sure she wouldn't get defensive at all. A cynical snort escaped from him as he thought about it. She had apologized to the little girl as they left—apologized for there being so much yelling. Her explanation was that their family had always been loud and full of opinions. She didn't take any responsibility. She didn't apologize for the weight her words had possibly just dropped upon her seven-year-old granddaughter.

"Daddy?"

"Yes, honey." His eyes shifted to the rearview mirror so he could see the little girl looking at him.

He would have to talk with her about what she heard. He owed her that, even though he wished he could just ignore it—hoped she could just forget.

"Do you remember my mom?" The question caught him off guard. It also hit him that the little girl had turned the woman who birthed her into a general noun rather than a proper noun. Had she always referred to her as "my mom"? Not just "Mom", almost as if she needed to be specific for him to know exactly who she was talking about—as though she was referring to a person who they didn't share.

Had he turned her into someone they didn't share?

"Yeah. Yeah, I do," he responded softly—unsure of what thought in her head inspired the question.

"You don't talk about her. I didn't know if you remembered her." Even if he knew what to say, he wasn't able to as a glob of guilt and despair filled his throat. He looked back at her. She was looking out at the window taking in the pleasant scenery as if she had just shared a common observation. He didn't know what to say. He didn't even know what he was capable of saying.

"Grandpa called Grandma a bitch."

The car jerked as his foot pushed on the brake in surprise at the matter-of-fact statement. The irony of his parents purposefully swearing at each other in a different language so their precious granddaughter wouldn't hear, and the fact they did it so often that she knew what they were saying anyway, released some of the mucus of emotion lodged in his throat.

"Well—yes. Yes, he did."

05/20/2016

The waterglass made a gentle thud on the table next to the couch, and Jo's hand closed around it before his fingertips even left the rim. Jo managed a thank you before her mouth gaped open with a sudden yawn which in turn made him yawn just as big and as sudden. Her legs swung up onto the couch as he sat on the connected chaise, feeling a sense of ease as he sat down for what felt like the first time that day.

"You're never going to get that glitter out the carpet."

He followed Jo's eyes to the middle of the living room where the cream-colored carpet now sparkled purple in one spot. He remembered the look on the little girls' faces as the tube of glitter—which had mysteriously made its way out of the dining room and into the living room—had fallen in an explosion of sparkling purple. Most of the faces looking in his direction had contained utmost fear, but the face of his daughter had gone from surprise to an apologetic grimace when meeting his eyes. Then they softened when she turned to the little girl whose loosened hand had caused the scene and whose bottom lip was starting to tremble.

"It's okay, Sophie. The floor is pretty now. We can clean it, right Daddy?" The steady young eyes had looked back to him for confirmation, along with a subtle challenging glint telling him that there was no need for it not to be okay. Once he had stopped holding his breath, he assured the frozen group of nine-year-olds that floors were in place to be walked on so getting it dirty wasn't a problem. Silently, he cursed himself for having not taken the carpet out of the living room.

He let out a sigh, still staring at the remnants of glitter that he was sure would in fact never detach from the carpet, and shrugged his shoulders. "The fact that the walls aren't solid glitter makes it a success to me. One spot isn't too bad."

"May the year of the tiger princesses never be forgotten," laughed Jo as she did a mock toast with her water. He laughed along with her.

"To the tiger princesses." He took a sip from his own glass, enjoying the carbonation of the soda and leaning his head back against the cushion.

Jo had been the first person he had called when he was informed that the preferred party theme this year would be tiger princesses. At first, he did some searching online trying to see if there was a reference he wasn't getting, but in fact, the idea had come straight from his daughter's mind and cemented itself with force. Jo had laughed when he called in a panic and provided the simple plan of going as literal as possible with it.

As the party guests showed up in their dresses, he and Jo had painted on their tiger faces—enacting a transformation before the little princesses could enter the forest kingdom living and dining room filled with fake greenery, green balloons and a couple blow up trees with monkeys hanging from them. It had been a hit, and the excited squeals that came from his daughter as she grabbed his hand shaking it up and down while jumping, meant everything. Gratitude for Jo filled him as he patted her foot next to him.

"It wouldn't have happened without you. You made her day."

"Anything for her," Jo said softly looking into her water before smirking at him. "I would have really liked to see what you could have come up with on your own though." He rolled his eyes.

"Sadist." He laid his head back and felt his eyelids comfortably close. "Thanks for coming out. I know it's a lot." His eyes popped open in realization. "You're the only friend who's been around since her first birthday." Lifting his head, he hoped it didn't sound as bitter as it had felt on the tail end of the thought. "I know everyone's busy with their own lives and it's a drive to get out here. I'm not blaming anyone. Life goes on."

Faces paraded through his mind of friends who had disappeared over time. Were they even friends anymore? He didn't know if friendships technically ended if they just faded away over time. Memories of a feeling wafted through the air, faint enough where he didn't feel them, but could recall the intense feeling of being forgotten—first by her and then over the next two years by the friends who had filled their lives before the baby. He had understood. People didn't know what to say, how he felt, what their role in his life was at that time. So they had slowly faded away. It would have been nice if that understanding also dissolved the pain—it hadn't, only time had been able to do that for him.

Jo's face was filled with her own thoughts when he looked over at her. She was never someone whose face was easy to read and always someone willing to share her thoughts whether solicited or not. A few wrinkles framed her unfocused eyes, and he was able to pick out a couple streaks of silver in her hair. Jo hadn't faded away but had stayed firm, refusing to be made into a memory despite the times she could have.

His tongue and throat went dry at the memory of standing in the hospital hallway with Jo a little over eight years ago. She had rushed at him with fearful energy, eyes red and wild, traveling from the door of the room to his face. He had felt her eyes burning through him even though he hadn't been feeling much of anything since the hospital had called him. Jo's eyes were so wide, and her face contorted by a panic that he was sure few had ever seen. Her hand had gripped onto his arm, the tips of her fingers burrowing into his muscle as she looked up at him with a plea for good news. News he didn't have.

"Braindead." The word came out with a voice he didn't recognize as his own. It was cracked and heavy yet faint as if there was not enough air to carry the words into existence. Jo's hand dropped and the panic left her with something resembling disbelief and realization of the worst kind. Her mouth hung open, eyes staring blankly at the door in front of them. He remembered seeing her face harden—her lips close.

"How did it get this bad?" she whispered icily.

He didn't know if her voice truly held the note of accusation he heard or if his mind had processed it to reflect his own deep feelings, but either way, it was if she had thrown a match on him—neither of them knowing that he was dry and covered in gasoline. He whipped toward her in a fierce glow of red—everything he had been trying to contain, and not even aware of, bubbling to the point of explosion within him.

"Maybe if you'd shown your face a little more it wouldn't have." The hallway had echoed with his snarled yell, taking all his breath from him and all the air within the walls surrounding them. Shock and fear filled Jo's eyes for one second before the rage shot right back at him—her lips becoming white with fury, barely moving as her voice stabbed at him.

"Fuck you."

The following motions happened in an instant as he felt something wet hit his face and watched her turn away, rushing down the hallway as quickly as she had come. It wasn't until she was completely gone that he remembered the feeling on his cheek and with a shaky hand wiped her spit off.

Regret and anger had torn at him for about a year after that until they had mutually hung their heads and she had come over to see the baby and talk over drinks. Tension had existed at the start of the conversation, but by the end they were in each other's arms, tears spilling down both their faces. Jo had been there for him and the little girl since—unwavering—coming out as often as she could and making the little girl's birthday party a weekend event where she would stay with them.

He looked forward to the birthday weekend as much as his daughter did. Having two late nights to talk and hang out with Jo brought him joy—no matter how high his mother would raise her eyebrow when he reminded her Jo would be staying at their house. He felt himself smirk a little, remembering the moment a few years ago when their hands touched each other in a different way right before their lips did. Both had pulled away after a moment—both making an unpleasant expression and then laughing, remarking how they felt they had just tried making out with a sibling.

Jo let out another yawn and gulped down the rest of her water before swinging her legs down.

"I'm done for the day. I'm going up to my room and getting some sleep, so I have energy for our breakfast tomorrow. She still likes the place on Hudson, right?" As he watched her get up, he started debating whether he wanted to move his body yet.

"Yeah, the 50's diner."

"Perfect," Jo said with a wink. "I wait all year for this weekend just for that priceless French toast."

01/27/2020

T he words *Beth (School Social Worker)* stared up at him from his phone and he answered with pleasant surprise.

"Hi, Beth." He smiled as she said his name and immediately asked how he was. He thought that it was in true social work fashion to begin a conversation by asking how someone was doing right away. He found it a refreshing break from the calls he usually took at work which often started with demands. "I'm doing pretty well, thank you. I do have to jump into a meeting in the next five minutes. I can talk for a couple minutes or call you back—"

"Oh, let me just get straight to the point then." Beth's voice was always soft and direct, which he had found very comforting since the first time talking to her. "I wanted to let you know that after my session with Avery today we talked about not having scheduled sessions anymore. She can still come to see me whenever she wants, but I'm not going to put any kind of expectation on it. It doesn't have to be weekly or biweekly anymore unless, of course, she wants to pop in that often." He felt himself deflate a little and knew that the slight concern was reflected in his voice.

"Really? Are you sure? She's been doing really well."

"You're right." Beth's voice was soft and energized at the same time. He could almost see her smile through the phone. "She is doing great. Avery has done an amazing job of walking through the things she was struggling with when she first saw me. She walked through them, overcame them, and knows what she can do in the future when any similar difficulties arise—which includes chatting with me or other people in her life. She has done fantastic and I'm so proud of her. I know I'm doing my job right when these kiddos don't really need me anymore." His heart lifted back up at her words.

His daughter was doing well—she was going to be okay. He couldn't ask for anything more.

"Thank you, Beth. For everything you've done for her—for us." His voice had become husky with emotion, and he found himself needing to clear his throat.

"She's the one who did the hard work. And you too by giving her the chance to do the work she needed to." Her words folded their arms around him, and he could feel the comforting warmth. Beth cleared her throat, and her voice took on a certain briskness. "But I'll let you get back to work. If you would like to talk through it at all, I should be available before five o'clock." His mouth began to form a response when her exclamation cut him short. "Oh, and I encourage you to ask Avery about her research paper."

"Her research paper?"

"The sixth-grade research paper is the big project for the year. See if she wants to share the topic she chose with you, or maybe see if she'll let you read the finished product," she advised, her words picking up in pace. "I'll let you go. Be well."

"Thank you, you too."

He looked down at the now silent phone trying to register all the thoughts in his brain. What could her research paper be about? Maybe he needed to be paying closer attention to her projects. Work had been busy recently and he knew sometimes he didn't ask the questions he needed to. A myriad of thoughts went through his mind as he walked into the meeting and sat down, only half-listening to the discussion.

One thought that he picked out of the many was that he was going to miss Beth. Even though her relationship had been primarily with Avery, she had been a lifeline for him – someone to whom he could hand over his girl and see that the hands taking her held in her in such a way that he could trust them completely. It had meant everything to him. It was as if he took a large gulp of water that had been handed to him and realized that all this time, he had been thirsty. He hadn't even realized that he had been feeling as if there was no one else who he could fully trust to have his child's best interest at heart, with no bias, no agenda, no expectations that were mismatched to who she is.

It had all started at the beginning of sixth grade. It was as if his little girl full of confidence and joy walked into the new building and walked out a different person. She had very quickly become more reserved and self-conscious. Suddenly, he didn't understand anything—or so she told him. Having friends over became more complex—what kind of extracurriculars she did or did not want to, or were suddenly unthinkable for her to participate in, became ever changing and contradictory. One time he had asked her if she wanted to come over to his coworker's house while they watched the football game, so she could play with his son whom she had played with several times before. Her eyes had stayed glued to the ground at his question.

"I can't," she whispered softly to her shoes.

"What?" he asked, genuinely confused by her answer wondering if he heard her right and, if so, then wondering if they had other plans he had forgotten about. The twelve-year-old eyes had suddenly glared up at him and he saw the flush on her cheeks, small fists balled up so tight they were turning white.

"I can't. I said I can't. I can't. I CAN'T, I CAN'T," her shrill voice exploded on him, and he stood frozen as she dashed out of the room in a rage. He stood there in shock for the longest time, trying to make sense of what had just happened and not getting to any kind of logical conclusion.

He remembered calling his sister and trying to explain how he didn't know what was happening—questioning if he had done something he wasn't aware of. He could practically hear his sister roll her eyes at him over the phone before she responded to him with dramatized annunciation.

"HORMONES."

He found his conversation with Jo to be a bit more helpful.

"Do you remember how middle school is the worst time of any human's life? It's just a mix of awkwardness, social hierarchy, puberty, changing in locker rooms, not to mention more kids than elementary school, and different than ones she spent the last five years with. Oh, and somewhere in there she's supposed to be learning too," Jo said dryly. "If she's not talking to you, see if she'll talk to someone who's available whenever she needs it." Jo's voice softened and he knew she felt guilty that she couldn't be that person. "See if the school has a counselor, or someone she can hash it out with."

The first time he met Beth, he liked her instantly. She directed most of her statements to the stiff little closed-up body next to him, which stared at her silently. Beth had made it clear that they could talk about whatever the child of stone wanted to talk about—those details of their conversations would remain between them, unless Avery expressed she was thinking about harming herself or others. He was grateful to see the young eyes widen at the remark as though she was surprised that someone would do such a thing. He felt himself start to breathe a little easier.

By the end of the conversation, he could see his daughter's body start to relax a little and when Beth said she could either leave with him or stay and talk just the two of them for a bit, the eyes brightened a little, though her voice was still hesitant as she said she'd stay and talk.

His daughter had started seeing Beth every day after lunch for half an hour and it didn't take long before he started to see the walls come down. Every week he would get a phone call from Beth explaining in a very general way some things they were working on and different ways he could work on supporting her. He remembered shaking his head one day in bewilderment.

"How do other parents just DO this?"

Beth was silent for a moment as if carefully choosing her words.

"Well, I think as parents we relate to our children through our own past experiences or the past experiences of others. I think for most kids usually one parent may be able to relate more in certain circumstances than the other. Not always, but sometimes. You're parenting her through situations and circumstances you did not experience. It's unknown territory and you have to know when to ask for help," said Beth softly. "The last part is something important for all of us on a parenting journey to remember. There are people who can help—even if it's not who we were expecting to have to reach out to when beginning this journey. It may not look how you thought it would and that's okay."

He had breathed a little easier.

Beth was the first person he called when he found the bloody underwear pushed down in the garbage can. His voice was panicked as she answered the personal number she had given him months ago, but he had yet to use.

"What does she need? What do I do? Why didn't she tell me? Can you tell me what to pick up from the store? And tampons are different sizes, right? How do I know which size will fit her? I'll have to show her, won't I? How to put it in. What? How? I don't know how to insert a tampon!" Beth didn't respond for a minute after his final exclamation, and he realized in hindsight she probably needed to compose herself after his hysterical outburst.

"First of all, you don't have to do this alone. She has a doctor, a school nurse, a grandmother, and a school social worker who all know how to insert a tampon. Also, there are instructions on the box which would be helpful for you to read just to increase your own knowledge." Her voice was calm and helpful even though he could detect a hint of laughter which he was starting to feel was appropriate. "A girl starting her period does not need to feel disgusted, shameful, or embarrassed by the natural process of her body. Girls don't need to feel more self-conscious about their existence than they're already made to feel. So, let's focus on that goal."

He had breathed a little easier.

He smiled down at his notepad in recollection. He knew there would be more to come—times where he would feel as though he was floundering through parenting his adolescent daughter, but Beth's calm voice seemed to be anchored within him. One sentence that had kept playing in his mind had startled him when she first said it. He wasn't even aware her voice was capable of carrying any explicit language, even though she had just been repeating a fear he had dramatically expressed during one of their first few phone calls. Her voice had somehow remained comforting though firm.

"How about we make a deal? If I think you're fucking up your kid, I'll let you know. And your end of the deal is to start believing the very true fact that you're not."

* * *

Avery's head bent low over her plate, her eyes going cross-eyed as she watched the noodle be sucked in between her lips. After her accomplishment was complete and the noodle completely disappeared, she smiled at him with pride as he smiled back at the line of sauce circling her lips. He looked back down at his own plate, twirling a noodle with his fork.

"So, any projects you're working on at school?" he asked casually glancing over at her as he stuck the noodle in his mouth. Her eyes narrowed at him, and she leaned back in her chair—her arms crossed with an attitude far beyond her years.

"You talked to Beth, didn't you?"

He feigned shock for one minute before giving her a shrug and nodding. "She told me I should ask about your research project. I didn't even know there was a big research project. Did I miss it somewhere or did you not tell me?" Her defensive front faded immediately, and she scooted back up to her plate spearing a clump of noodles with her fork.

"I might have mentioned having to do some research, but I didn't say much else," she said, shrugging as if this was normal. He felt himself furrow his eyebrows. They talked about most of her schoolwork, and she was typically excited to share new things she learned or a project she was working on. He couldn't decide whether to push the issue or not.

Was there a reason she didn't want to talk about this research paper? He couldn't imagine why. His eyes went back down to his noodles as they sat in silence for a few minutes, him waiting to see if she would just continue on without any prodding. A slight annoyance took hold as he looked over and saw her watching him expectantly as she slurped in another noodle.

"You could just provide more information without me asking for it, you know," he lightly grumbled at her. She responded with a smile, though somewhat hesitant.

"Maybe I'm not sure what you want to know," she replied. He raised his eyebrows and tilted his head. There was never a time when he didn't want to know anything she was willing to share. And she knew it.

The almost-teenager threw him a sigh of surrender as she let her fork clatter onto her plate. "Okay, I'll show you the draft."

She got down from her chair and ran to the front door where she had left her backpack. He found himself somewhat nervous to see what it was, now that it had been built up. It wasn't long before he saw the paper land on the table out of the corner of his eye as she slid back into her chair looking at him cautiously. He smiled at her—hoping to relieve her apparent concerns. As his eyes dropped down to the paper next to him, he found himself reading the bold typed words out loud before fully registering them.

"Postpartum depression." He read the words again, once in his head and another time out loud, not finding a clear answer. He knew what it was, but—why?

She was looking at him expectantly, and he didn't know what she was expecting. "That's an interesting research topic. What made you choose that?" Her look didn't change, as though he was asking her a question she thought he already knew the answer to.

"Because of—because of my mom," Avery hesitantly whispered.

It was like a punch in the chest. Not because of what she said, but because of how she said it—as if he would be angry or sad or disappointed or respond with some other kind of negative reaction. It surprised him—he realized for several reasons.

"Why did you think you couldn't tell me?" he asked softly and watched as her shoulders lifted toward her ears, her voice still hesitant.

"I didn't want to make you sad or think about her if you didn't want to." Her eyes rested on her plate; her hands invisible under the table.

"Avery." She looked up at him as though she was still expecting him to have a massive mental breakdown. His heart filled with love for her—his girl who cared so much even to a fault. "You are never responsible for what I feel and you are always allowed to bring up your mom, no matter how I might react. That's my problem to deal with if it makes me feel a certain way—never yours. You know that, right?" Her body softened and the air of concern seemed to fade away.

"I know, Dad. I just didn't know if you would like the topic. Aunt Jo said it's probably what mom had and why—why she left."

He pushed the slight frustration he felt at Jo for

not telling him they had been talking about her aside. It wasn't important anyway; he was confident Jo wouldn't have said anything he wouldn't have said himself.

This wasn't a new conversation, but it had been a very general one. Partly because he wasn't sure what to say, and also because he wasn't exactly sure what had happened. Certain assumptions had been made which were probably close to the truth, but he had accepted that the actions leading up to her death were unknown. It had taken years for him to get to that place as an adult. How was a twelve-year-old supposed to come to terms with that? He read the words staring up at him again. Maybe she was further along than he thought. He felt himself go into an instinctual prayer—*God, please help me to show up how my daughter needs me to.*

"Yeah, she went to the doctor and fit some of the symptoms for—that." He flinched, slightly ashamed that he couldn't say the words. *God, please help me show up how my daughter needs me to.* "For postpartum depression. Was there a specific reason you wanted to learn more about it?" He could imagine the answer was obvious as his daughter gained a little more confidence, showing some eagerness to share her explanation. For a little under twelve years, his little girl had gone through life without the one person most people had in their lives. It would make sense to want to understand why.

"Beth and I had been talking about it and she thought maybe I should learn about it. So, I started doing research, and then I realized I could just do my research project on it. I could learn about it and do a research project that was important." He was surprised by what seemed to be excitement in her voice. Her eyes took on a shine that was more familiar to him than the girl he had been staring at just a few minutes ago. "And I've really learned a lot." He smiled at her and stuck his last forkful of noodles into his mouth.

"Like what?" The noodles slipped comfortably down his throat. She was looking directly at him, a soft smile on her lips filled with genuine joy which was also reflected in her eyes and carried through her voice as she spoke.

"Like it wasn't my fault."

Not a single thought entered his mind before he was next to her chair, wrapping his arms around her and kissing the top of her head. Every ounce of love poured from him and surrounded her, pushing aside the guilt and sadness that crept in at the thought of her ever-having thought otherwise. His hand cupped her cheek, now damp with tears, as he felt her let go against his chest.

"No, baby girl, it wasn't. It wasn't anyone's fault."

01/27/1979

T he air stung the tops of her ears—the prickling sensation slowly traveled from the top of her cartilage to the soft lobe. She felt herself prickle back at the air in response, looking around disgruntledly at the cloud-covered sky and the bare trees reaching up to it. She involuntarily shivered and felt her nose wrinkle in irritation and distaste.

"I hate winter. It's cold and ugly." Her papa looked over at her in a quiet response—his eyes slightly amused, but the rest of his face blank.

"Ugly?" She watched him look over the land that lay in front of them, his eyes looking over the dried stems of wildflowers surrounded by brown-tinged grass and then up to the naked trees slightly shivering in the subtle wind. Her eyes joined his and she took it all in again, feeling reassured in her assessment: ugly. "What do you think makes it ugly?" Her papa spoke softly in a low comforting hum.

"Everything looks dead," she blurted out and

199

knocked the toe of her purple boot, which hung off the edge of the porch, into some of the browning grass. One of the longer stems cracked at the unexpected impact and the broken top half hung haphazardly as if providing a solid example of her exclamation. She looked back to her papa who had noticed her destruction with a blank face.

Wrinkles surrounded his eyes and mouth interrupting the smooth leathery skin of his cheeks. She liked his wrinkles. They made her feel safe looking into his face. His face was soft and old—the way she knew her papa to look. Upon further inspection, she noticed that his hair was almost all a dark silver, pulled back into a loose ponytail with strands of black weaving in and out of the lighter hairs. She thought there was more silver than when they came to the ranch last year. Would he be all silver someday? She didn't know anyone with all silver hair. She liked the idea of her papa's hair being silver. It matched his soft wrinkles.

He spoke in his language making the hum of his voice even deeper and richer. Naturally, as if he had spoken in English, she warmed at him calling her "little bird".

"Never is everything dead." His hand felt heavy and warm on the top of her head as he smoothed down her hair. "What makes you think they are dead?" Papa asked with his hand motioning to the trees standing against the sky and the tall grass swaying in the breeze. She felt her confidence in her previous exclamation wane, but she looked at the land before her, taking in the browns and grays.

"All the green is gone. There are no leaves on the trees anymore." She felt her nose instinctually crinkle again as she pointed at the grass. "And everything is boring brown. Dead and boring."

The rich laughter that came from her papa surprised her and automatically made her smile. She liked his face when he laughed as it softened and folded even more, the depth of his wrinkles growing. His eyes continued to laugh even after his mouth stopped.

"I'm not sure that I would say death is boring, little bird." She watched him look to the sky, close his eyes, and breathe in deeply. She wondered if he was breathing in the same cold air she was. He seemed to taste it. She opened her mouth and breathed in deeply too, feeling the chill enter her lungs with a crispness. It felt like air. Her papa seemed to be breathing in more.

His eyes popped back open, and his long arm reached around her—pulling her comfortably close against him, her head resting comfortably under his armpit.

"Do you know why the trees drop their leaves?" She gazed at the tall dark trunks and the thin reaching branches.

"No, Papa. Don't the leaves just die and fall?" She looked at the trees and their bare bodies, wondering if they were cold in the wind. She felt a twinge of sadness as she thought out loud. "Poor trees, all their leaves are so pretty and then they lose them." She could see leaves speckled throughout the grass, darker shades of brown, contorted and crumpled. Could the trees see them—their beautiful leaves dead on the ground? She hoped they couldn't. Worry struck her. But certainly, the trees could feel the loss of their leaves.

"Do not worry, little bird," Papa said as if her worry pulsated through her body, and he could hear the vibrations. His thick arm gently squeezed her body against his. "The trees do not lose their leaves—they let them go."

"They let them go?" It was slightly uncomfortable for her to swivel her head back so she could see his face, but she wanted to see her papa's face. His face seemed to hold answers and explanations. Maybe that's why he had wrinkles—to hold all the answers.

Papa looked down at her and smiled, his soft hand brushed against her cheek with warmth for a moment. She regretfully looked back down as her neck muscles protested at her looking straight up into his face any longer. When he spoke, she noticed she could feel the hum of his words through his chest. Had she ever felt words before?

"The trees let the leaves go so they can survive the winter and conserve their water. Do you know what conserve means?"

"Yes," she said confidently, but at the same time questioned herself. Did she know what it meant or was she thinking of another word? Papa's arm gently squeezed her again.

"It means to not waste any water or use it in a way not needed." She hadn't known what conserve meant. "So instead of feeding water to the leaves, the trees keep all the water they can in their roots—keeping the whole tree alive and allowing leaves to bud in the coming Spring." She felt her eyes widen at his explanation as she looked at the trees so bare and naked.

"Wow, Papa. The trees just know how to do that without us telling them to?" Her eyes took in a solid dark trunk shooting out from the prairie grass and followed it up to where the trunk turned into thick branches and kept spreading and reaching through more and more branches. She realized she was never able to see how many branches there really were on a single tree when it was covered with leaves. "Trees are smart, Papa, aren't they?"

"They are very smart. They do not need to learn from us, little bird—we learn from them." She looked up at Papa who was also staring out at the trees. She turned her eyes back to them and stared at them with puzzlement, waiting for them to start talking to her like one of her teachers in front of the classroom. They stayed standing and silent. Her puzzled gaze turned back to her papa.

"I can't hear them, Papa. How can they teach if they can't talk?"

"Hmph." The pleasant sound came from his chest like a laugh that had stayed silent until the very end. "One of the best ways we learn is from what we see rather than what we're told. The trees teach us every fall and winter when they let their leaves fall. The falling leaves are the lessons, little bird."

Her eyes spotted the lessons he was referring to throughout the grass, but they still just looked like leaves to her. An urge to run out and grab a leaf to see if something was written on it gripped her. She'd seen leaves before, there was never writing on them. Maybe it was written in the language of the trees and she just didn't know how to read it. She looked back up at her papa, catching the underside of his chin which was covered in small dots of newly growing silver and black hair. Papa could probably read the language of the trees.

"What is the lesson?"

"Through different seasons, the trees' priorities, or what is important to them changes. In Spring, they grow, pushing their energy out through the branches to the new buds to make the leaves you find so beautiful." He smiled down at her, his large hand gently covering her forearm. She was bundled up in his arm and against his chest, no longer aware of the chill in the air.

"And in the winter the trees realize that what is important changes as does where their energy is needed. If they saw continued growth the most important thing, then they would run out of energy when winter comes and there is less water and nutrients available. So, they let go of their leaves.

Even if the leaves make them beautiful to the eyes of others and they put so much into letting the leaves grow, they know that keeping water in their roots will help them to live during the winter seasons of their lives. They also know draining the soil of water to try and keep their leaves doesn't help their brother and sister trees stay alive either. The trees adjust to the seasons instead of fighting them or trying to make the seasons be something they're not."

Her papa's strong arms reached under her own smaller ones and easily lifted her into his lap. She giggled at the weightless feeling of being momentarily picked up. Her parents would tell her she was too big for them to pick her up anymore. It made her happy that she wasn't too big for Papa's arms.

"The trees teach us that through life what is

important to us can change, how we nurture ourselves and our loved ones—" his fingers gently drummed on her stomach, and she giggled at the tinkle of his light touch, "changes with the seasons we go through. There are times for growth and the obvious beauty it brings, but there are also times to let go and only hold on to what keeps you standing." He brought his mouth close to her ear and his breath was warm as it whispered in it.

"Even if a young passerby thinks it may look ugly."

She gave him a shrewd look knowing he was talking about her, but it disappeared at his responsive smile. "If we try to ignore the seasons and ignore how our needs are affected by them, we run out of what allows us to have moments of bloom in the first place."

She caught the finality in his words as she continued to look out over the sea of grass and looked up with admiration at the dark trees that were smart enough to be teachers to humans. The slight breeze moved through the grass causing ripples, and she saw the smaller branches of the trees come to life with a wave. The large trunk of the tree stayed still. Immovable. Solid.

She had seen pictures of trees' roots before and imagined them all underground gently cradling the soil filled with water and the nutrients Papa had talked about. She wondered if she had unseen roots in her—holding on with care to whatever Papa had talked about people needing.

"Do you understand, little bird?" Papa asked softly, the light pressure of his chin resting on the top of her head changing with the formation of his words.

"I don't know, Papa," she said softly, knowing that he wouldn't be frustrated with her, or she wouldn't be wrong for not understanding. His arms squeezed her tightly in response and she relaxed further into his hold.

"That is okay, my little bird. Maybe someday you will."

Epilogue

T he microphone was close enough that if I
    stuck out my tongue, I would be able to
feel the crisscross texture and taste the metal.
Looking down my nose at it, I gave the assertive
device a nervous look of distaste. A small smile
snuck out of my mind and onto my face when
remembering how Jennifer had sputtered into
her water with a laugh. It had been somewhat
comical when her assistant had directed me to keep
pulling the microphone closer and closer—and still
closer—until I had exasperatedly asked if she just
wanted me to swallow it.

A sense of relief filled me as I noticed that the
prickling nerves that had begun to bounce around
in my stomach also seemed to have snuck out. Jennifer caught my eye as she adjusted her headphones
and microphone while saying something to her
producer before directing her voice to me.

"We're going to start in a minute," Jennifer
warned. "Last chance for a last-minute nervous pee

break." I smiled at her while also taking a reactive assessment of my bladder.

"I think I'm good. I did my best to limit my coffee despite your assistant being very generous with all the beverage options." Jennifer's eyes lit up in excitement.

"You'll have to let her make you something before you go. She's a freaking wizard with that coffee machine." She stopped herself from any further excited explanation and sat up alert, pointing to her headphones and giving me a slight nod that I read as *it's go-time.* "I'm going to intro and we're on. Ready?"

"As I'll ever be," I replied, crossing my arms in front of me and leaning in a little more. Jennifer's podcast was one of my favorites to be on—not only because it was the first one I felt confident doing a couple years ago, but because she kept her expectations low and let the content be the content. It had a familiar rhythm of how I tended to structure, or destructure, my own sessions.

Jennifer's podcast had also continued to grow, and she typically asked for shorter segments from professionals so she could get to numerous segments in her hour and a half episode. Seeing an email that only requested about fifteen minutes of me talking was always a relief. I slowly tuned back into Jennifer's words as I heard my name.

"And so now we're going to hear from one of my favorite guests to join us for a quick Wednesday chat. She is a clinical psychologist who has worked with a multitude of different populations, but currently specializes in perinatal mental health and parenting—Dr. Avery Blehmiski, hello!" I smiled back at Jennifer as her eyes lit up and she gave me wink.

"Hi, Jennifer. I'm so happy to be back and for your invitation to have a casual conversation about meaningful stuff." I noticed how Jennifer very subtly moved her swivel chair back and forth, back and forth—unable to keep herself completely still when she was in her element.

"Well, we're old friends here by now and so I know you won't mind if we just skip some of the pleasantries and jump into it."

"Let's do it," I replied feeling my shoulders loosen and lower as my body began to have its automatic response of confidence.

"Most of the women and parents you see come to you in a crisis, correct? Or in a problematic state, if crisis is too extreme of a word?" My mind registered her words and my own words flowed out without thought.

"I think problematic state is a good way to put it, but for many people, a problematic state in parenthood can very much feel like a crisis. And therefore, it should be considered a crisis, even if another parent may categorize the experience as just another Tuesday. That's one of the first things I want to make sure people realize when they come to meet with me—we're going to talk about their experience and their experience—their crisis—is valid and not comparable to another person's experience. Every struggle is valid."

"I feel like I know the answer to this question, but do you meet with parents who are proactively seeking services? Prevention versus crisis management?"

"No. Not only is proactive mental health treatment, counseling—whatever you want to call it—not common in general across the board of people seeking help, but especially with parents. The stigma that still surrounds mental health struggles, diagnoses, and treatment is strong. I don't think I'm wrong in saying that the stigma surrounding counseling for parents is even stronger." I could feel my voice begin to rise with passion, reminding myself to take it down a notch. I could hear my dad remind me, "the loudest voice isn't always the one that's heard the best".

"I know you're going to tell us why, but for the sake of asking—why? Why is there such a stigma and barrier for parents to get help with parenting and their own mental health?" I leaned back slightly and noticed how I had uncrossed my arms at some point and had most likely been moving around while I was talking. I needed to make sure not to knock the microphone inconveniently placed in the line of fire.

"Because of the messaging surrounding parenthood, specifically motherhood, and the kind of expectations that society sets for parents." I swiveled my chair slightly to the side so my uncontrolled flailing arms weren't as dangerous. "Let's stick with mothers for a moment. When meeting with these women, I have to be aware of the lingering societal message they hear, which is, if you're a woman you should be a natural mother. Even though this message isn't as loud as it used to be in our society, it's still there. A woman is still expected to be a mother—even if the alternative is more accepted. So, these women hear that external message internally as *motherhood should be natural for me, so if it's hard or I feel I'm failing—there is something fundamentally wrong with me.*" I saw Jennifer nod as I talked, and then her brow furrow as she considered her responding thought.

"And this is something that needs to be challenged because so much of what is deemed natural in motherhood, really just isn't," she exclaimed, her arm movement matching my own.

"Exactly," I responded, seeing the wheels in her

head start turning quicker.

"I can easily relate that to my own experience of breastfeeding, which I've shared on here before. I have breasts," Jennifer gestured to her chest while looking at the microphone as though addressing the audience. "And I had a baby, and these breasts of mine are naturally supposed to produce milk. So, imagine my surprise when, after multiple visits with lactation consultants, I was still unable to produce enough breastmilk to feed my baby for six months before he ended up needing to supplement with formula anyway." Jennifer sat back from her excited state and looked at me. I could see her remembering the struggle, the consultations, the pumping, the raw nipples, the tears of her own and her son's as she just tried to feed him. "There was a lot of guilt in that," she said softly and I jumped on the word as if an electric shock went through my body.

"Yes, that's what a lot of women and parents experience. Guilt, shame, sadness—all due to the idea that what should have been natural or what is shown as easy, wasn't for them. And for many people, it's not easily shrugged off as *this didn't work that way for me and that's okay* or *I had a different experience from you because it was my experience and that's okay.* The amount of external and internal pressure put on parenthood often leaves people not able to get to those conclusions and believe them on their own." Jennifer's head had been nodding along and her mouth opened as I took a breath.

"So, when working with parents are you focusing mainly on these messages that they've adopted into their own thinking?"

"Most of the time, yes, that's the main focus of what we look at. We can even start by looking at the language used when talking with parents or how parents phrase their sentences when discussing difficulties they have. Often the phrase *but I love them* or, *but I wouldn't trade it for the world* are used almost out of reaction. You can tell me that eating a meal with your toddler is the worst part of your day and you hate it. Period. You shouldn't feel that your love for your child is then in question just because you don't like aspects of parenthood or that you don't like aspects of your child." I heard my voice get higher with emphasis as I threw my arms up and Jennifer smiled nodding along.

"For one, as an outside person, it's not even my right to question whether or not you love your child. And we as people should not put parents in the position of having to prove that they love their children enough or in the right way." Jennifer made a rolling motion with two of her fingers and I smiled happily letting the words keep flowing from my mind.

"We have to reframe the mindset that so many people have about what makes someone a good parent or a bad parent. So many people are filled with the idea of the *shoulds.* Filled with *they should do this if they're a good parent* and then *they shouldn't do that if they're a good parent* and it's a constant wheelhouse of just trying to fit into a standard that we don't even necessarily question all the time.

For one thing, there's the idea that if you're a parent you should be one hundred percent grateful that you're a parent one hundred percent of the time, otherwise you must not love your kid. And it's that kind of thinking that results in this unrelenting guilt and shame that parents typically don't know what to do with. So, you have people struggling—just trying to figure out what they're supposed to do—how to do this thing that isn't really talked about. Plus, they're trying to do it with very little coping skills when it comes to going through a huge transitional process of losing identity, shifting into another identity, and having someone depend on you the way you've never had someone depend on you before.

And of course, this is all occurring along with unsolicited input and judgment from others. And we haven't even started talking about hormones yet! Add in hormonal imbalances which occur regularly in women postpartum—a difficult situation

215

is turned into a seemingly impossible one." I took a breath and grabbed a cup of water that I just noticed sitting next to me as Jennifer silently applauded. The cool water moistened my tongue getting rid of the odd feeling that my tongue was going to trip over itself.

"What about parents who aren't showing up well? Those who have come to you through child services—who have crossed lines that many of us can't imagine crossing as parents? What is your response to them or how do you work with them?"

"Some of the parents who come to me for help have done what we call *the unthinkable*. They've laid their hands on their kids; they've screamed profanities at them with complete rage; they've walked out and not wanted to come back. These are the quote unquote, unthinkable things that," my fingers went up automatically motioning quotation marks, "*bad* parents might do." I paused looking down into the microphone and then back up to Jennifer's expectant face.

"And this is my question—how is that unthinkable? Have you ever been screamed at by an infant or a toddler endlessly? Have you ever been sleep-deprived to the point where you are no longer in control of your reactions? Have you ever been in these situations and not had outside support or any internal coping skills for how to react in a possibly more appropriate way? I want to question why this is seen as unthinkable. Because without emphasis on postpartum mental health, without emphasis on emotional support during what is an extreme life transition, it really makes sense that these reactions occur.

Despite love, despite how much they care about the child, there's not much else they're given. Especially if we're talking about parents who lack the external support of family who can help them or financial ability to have their child in daycare or hire someone to watch their child. For some reason, external support and coping skills are truly just a luxury within our society. Parents are not just automatically given those things. They are a luxury if they have access to them." I took another breath and stared into the metal mesh of the microphone.

"That is what's unthinkable."

* * *

"Oh, you are right. It doesn't matter how many damn features are on that Nespresso, it's got nothing on this," Jennifer said as she took a sip out of the glass coffee mug. I watched her eyes dance around the shop taking in all of its eccentricities. "I'm pretty sure I've been in here before. I just don't take a whole lot of time to sit for coffee, you know?" I took a sip from my own cup feeling the warm caramel flavor swirl around in my mouth, and smiled at the hint of lavender, as the liquid smoothly flowed down my throat. "Is this a favorite place of yours?" asked Jennifer looking at her own drink in appreciation.

"My dad used to take me here whenever we would come into the city. He was close with the past owner." I looked behind the dark wooden counter where the baristas took orders and swirled around each other in a dance of pouring, steaming, and frothing. From what I could tell by the pictures, a great deal of the shop had stayed the same since Jo sold it about fifteen years ago and started her world travels. "I try and make it a point to come in every now and then, so I can give a report to him. Let him know one of his favorite spots is still standing."

"Does your dad still live around here?"

"Yeah." I looked out the window at the cars passing by, slowly weaving in and out of each other in a contradictory hurried way. "Well, outside of the city where I grew up. He was finally convinced by my mom to travel seasonally. They have a place in the mountains they travel to for a few months out of the year."

"Hmm, some parents never stop putting aside their own desires, do they? Even when the kids have been gone for over ten years." Jennifer lifted an eyebrow at me and took another sip of her coffee while shaking her head. I wondered if it was one of her parents or a grandparent that my dad reminded her of.

"It's a hard habit to break. Another difficult shift of identity during aging, which has its own fun little mental twists for most people," I responded with a smile. Maybe it was her—a glimpse of a future self she desperately did not want to become. I rolled my eyes internally at myself. She wasn't asking to be analyzed.

"And let me guess, your mom was done with her caregiving duties and ready to travel before you even left for college," Jennifer smirked at me.

"She actually got me as a bonus child when I was sixteen, so I'm guessing she wouldn't have minded if the caregiving stage lasted a little longer," I replied watching the glint of Jennifer's journalistic eyes react to my words, knowing there was a story to be told. I was glad to see her put her interviewer hat aside as she looked back down at her coffee then back up at me with a more subdued look. "She just really wanted my dad to be happy without holding himself back. And he's always loved the mountains."

We both let the words breathe as we sipped our coffee. I thought of my dad on the deck of the cabin, reading a book and listening to the birds in the trees—every now and then looking up from the pages and leaning his head back, eyes straight to the sky—just pausing. I had never asked what those pauses were for—if they were for anything.

"So." Jennifer's voice broke my train of thought. "Is this the day I convince you to write a book?" I let out a snort which made her laugh. "It would be great, come on. You can't tell me you haven't thought more about it," she exclaimed eagerly. I shook my head. I should have expected her to bring it up again, but it hadn't been on my radar. She looked at me with exaggerated exasperation. "Come on, just a short one."

"You're basically asking me to have another baby, and let me tell you, I'm set with the two I have." I had barely entertained the idea the first time she brought it up—having just gotten to a place of following what I tell my own clients by putting down the plates I couldn't hold in my hands instead of trying to balance them on my head.

"I'm in a spot where my client load doesn't result in a crazy schedule, I get to enjoy my sons and I'm actually not too exhausted to have a relationship with myself and with my husband. That is a precious spot." Jennifer nodded in understanding, but I could see the slight disappointment in her eyes. "Let's just say, I'm not saying no and I'm not saying yes. Just not now."

Jennifer rolled her eyes dramatically as she finished another sip of coffee. "You psychologists and all your self-assertive yet non-committal words."

I smiled at her and enjoyed the words repeating themselves in my head. Not now. There was comfort in a possibility staying just a possibility, and enjoyment in the present being allowed to just be. A soft beeping interrupted my internal mantra and I looked at the watch on my wrist recognizing the notification without having to read it.

"I have an appointment in forty-five minutes. I should get going so I have time to settle in before it starts." I took a final gulp to drain my cup. "Sorry to ditch you."

Jennifer waved her hand dismissing my apology as I grabbed my bag from the floor next to the chair and stood up.

"Just a quick question, Avery." I looked up from my bag back to Jennifer's face, which had shifted to one of timid questioning. Her thumb nervously rubbed the handle of the coffee mug, and I could tell she was biting the inside of her lip. It was hard to believe that I was looking at the same confident, award-winning author and podcaster with whom I had just spent over an hour watching command her business.

Except, really, it wasn't that hard to believe.

Jennifer glanced back up at me with some hesitancy before she spoke again. "Do you ever feel unsure that you're doing any of it right?"

A small chill went down my spine as the quiet thought wisped across my mind: had she ever sat in this same shop and asked that same question?

I sat back down in the chair across from Jennifer who was looking at me desperately – her eyes begging for a kind of validation she probably rarely received from the people she needed to hear it from. My fingers gently touched the back of her hand which had been tensing instinctually. At my touch, I felt it soften.

"All the time."

* * *

"I feel so disconnected from her and I don't want to be. I don't want to be disconnected. I don't want to be a bad mom. I want to love her." I saw the women's eyes widen in horror at her own words, looking directly at me suddenly—seeing if I heard them too. Pleading desperation entered her voice. "I do love her. I do love her! I just never wanted to be this kind of mom. It's just all too hard. I just can't do it."

222

The women's arms were wrapped around her own body as she instinctually tried to comfort herself. I felt my own body soften toward her, leaning forward as though being pulled to reach out to her.

"Erin. You are not a bad mom. You don't get to use that term for yourself in this room again. You are a mom experiencing parts of motherhood that you weren't expecting. Parts of parenthood are left out of the parenting books sometimes. It is hard and you need help which is why you walked into my office. I'm so proud of you for taking that step. And, Erin—" I scooched myself to the very edge of my chair, unable to resist extending my arm as far as I could to grab the woman's desperately limp hand. I felt her whole body shudder at my touch as if able to slightly let go of being everything for itself and everyone else. "You're not alone."

Her red-rimmed green eyes looked up at mine, less wild, soft tears welling up just above the bottom lid and flowing out of the outside corner of her eye into single droplets on each side of her face. I knew these droplets were filled with the guilt, filled with the fear, the exhaustion, the anger, the grief, the relief. As another round of tears fell, I felt her hand gain strength and cling onto mine.

It was in that instant—it happened.

It had happened many times before, but each time

was just as startling and mesmerizing as the first time.

The green eyes staring into mine were not Erin's. They were the eyes of a woman from thirty years ago. The eyes of a woman who had tried to make love be enough and carry her through. They were the eyes of a woman who had shattered and had given the shattered pieces of herself away before realizing they were meant for her and her alone—never meant to be given away but only shared. They were the eyes of the woman who had held me and loved me.

They were the eyes of my mother.

I looked into those eyes with my very heart—my very soul—through tears slight enough that they would not fall. Her hand was warm in mine as my grip tightened ever-so-slightly so she could feel my words.

"This is not your fault. You are not bad." And you are not alone.

Author's Notes

In writing this book, I purposefully left the two main characters without names or much physical description. It was my hope that in doing so, the emphasis would not be on the character's themselves but on the experiences they are walking through. My intent was to make the emotions and thoughts as relatable as they could be for those who would relate, and avoid any barriers that well-defined characters could create.

Awareness of perinatal disorders continues to grow, but many people are still left unprepared, especially when their experience presents differently than stereotypical depressive symptoms. Below are resources if you or someone you know needs to reach out for help:

Postpartum Support International

- Support Helpline: (800)944-4773

- Text en Espanol: (971)203-7773
- Website : www.postpartum.net

National Alliance on Mental Illness

- Helpline: (800)950-6264
- Crisis Text line: text "NAMI" to 741741
- Website: www.nami.org

National Suicide Prevention Lifeline (English and Spanish): (800)273-8255

About the Author

Kelleen Goerlitz is a writer, poet, playwright and author of *Consumed by a Season*. Growing up, she had storylines and streams of words flowing through her mind before she could even put pencil to paper legibly. Her writing over the past fifteen years has focused on observations of the human experience - capturing the beauty of truth, and the struggle to find it, through playlets, poems, and fictional stories. The theme of her writing continues to grow with her, but stays true to her own struggles and triumphs while experiencing the fullness of life. Out of a passion for writing and a desire to let her work be shared with others, Kelleen Goerlitz recently began her journey as a self-published author with further work of different varieties yet to come.

You can connect with me on:

- 🌐 https://www.kelleengoerlitz.com
- *ℓ* https://www.instagram.com/kgoerlitzwriting

Also by Kelleen Goerlitz

The Complete Works of a Lost Girl

The Complete Works of a Lost Girl is a collection of playlets and poems which capture the beauty, tragedy, tension and freedom that is the human experience. This work contains seven playlets ranging from a Greek tragedy to dystopian fiction and sixteen poems of different styles. Over a decade ago the words which make up this body of work were given a voice and encouraged to find their way out of a tumultuous mind and flow out into the world through the tip of a pen. They may be imperfect, but in their imperfection they are true to the mind which created them and the heart which gave them life.

Made in the USA
Middletown, DE
05 March 2022